S0-AGP-832

The Fishermen's Ball
by J. J. Dutra

Fair Winds

Judy Dutra

Copyright © 2015 J.J. Dutra

All Rights Reserved

ISBN–10: 0996461701

ISBN-13: 9780996461702 (Judith J. Dutra)

CreateSpace, North Charleston, South Carolina

This book is a work of fiction. Some events are real, but the characters portrayed, together with their actions and statements are freely interpreted and are not intended precisely to depict actual persons. Names of boats and businesses are used fictitiously and any character resembling persons living or dead is a coincidence. The ideas, words and story are a product of the author's over-active imagination.

On the cover, the block print, *A Provincetown Flounder Dragger* is by Charles Kaeslau (1889-1972). It was donated as the cover illustration for the booklet for the Provincetown Fishermen's Association 'First Anniversary Ball' in 1937. The artist lived in Provincetown for twenty-two years.

Acknowledgements

Thank you to the many people who have encouraged me to write, especially Mary Hutchings-Snider, Bev Phaneuf and Angela Caruso who first read the book, knew it needed lots of work, but loved it anyway.

To Emily Bunker, editor of the highest order, thank you for being so honest, helpful and so knowledgeable.

To the Provincetown History Preservation Project Committee and Provincetown Portuguese Festival Committee, many thanks for maintaining the stories and heritage of Provincetown.

The Provincetown Advocate archives supplied ambience and local color.

Thanks too to Kevin Cotter for the book layout and design help.

The National Weather Service provided me multiple facts about the September 21, 1938 hurricane.

Much inspiration came from listening to the music of Glenn Miller, Tommy Dorsey and Duke Ellington.

Thanks mostly to my #1 fan, Dave, for understanding my need to write.

The book, *The Fishermen's Ball* is dedicated to Katherine & Frederick Jahnig, Herman & Juliana Dutra and Patricia Morris — gone but not forgotten.

Prologue

The sun was well below the horizon when Alonzo made his move. The drunken ravings of the captain, shipmates who kept to themselves, and the sounds from behind locked cabin doors from people no one would talk about, had coalesced, making this crossing a trip from hell. High seas had forced the trawler to take refuge inside the peninsula. There was always danger when out at sea, but now Alonzo was taking a calculated risk. He judged it to be a short swim to the dory that lay thirty yards from the stern of the trawler bobbing on its anchor, just waiting to take him to shore. Earlier that day he'd watched the fishing boats coming back to port, tying to the many piers that protruded from the land like fingers on a beckoning hand. The merchant ship would head north with the turn of the tide to unload the last of its cargo in Portland, Maine before heading back to France. Alonzo scanned the horizon. He had made a decision.

The harbor was wide and open. The town was low lying, nestled tightly, and facing the bay. He watched boats pass one another, some with lights on at the mast, white at the top, green on the starboard, and red to port. There were vessels of all sizes on moorings as well as tied to the wharfs and docks. He had a plan and was now eager to be off this ship. The wind was picking up, slapping waves against the metal hull, making enough noise to cover his escape over the side, down a hawser, and into the cold water that would carry him to a new life.

He planned to persevere and disappear into this town bordered by water and dunes.

There was always a chance that the mate in the wheelhouse might look his way and set off an alarm, but it was too late to turn back. He knew it would be hours before the change of watch. No one except the first mate had reason to care that he was gone. The captain wouldn't turn around for one lost crewman, of that he was sure. He smiled and patted the hem of his coat, as if all the answers to his problems were held there. His experience on the sea and the two stolen coins gave him the impetus to start over. And now he no longer had a choice. Determination and arrogance drove him forward and down. The hardest part came first: a swim in deep water to the skiff. After that he would row some distance. Then he would walk the sand flats that stretched a quarter of a mile to the dry beach. It didn't look far. Slipping into the liquid his body felt the shock of cold. He was pursued by guilt and fear as he swam for his life.

Alonzo thought about the water of is childhood home on San Miguel. It was the largest island in a chain of volcanic rocks protruding from the deep trenches off the west coat of Africa, the Western Isles, known as the Azores. The water of this harbor was colder. There were no mountain peaks above the skyline in this place, only one solitary monolith, like an Egyptian obelisk, towered above the village.

The forty-five degree seawater weighted him with a palpable force, restraining his movements as he worked to lift his arms and push his legs. His clothing expanded, pulling him down. He fought the current, the cold, and a desire to give up. His journey began with this swim to the double-ended dory that he had spotted earlier from the stern of the freighter. His rapid breaths came in puffs of vapor. Time slowed as if this were part of a dream, taking hours instead of minutes before he touched the side of the small boat. His muscles twitched in spasms as he threw his arms over the wooden rail. He needed to hurry. The cold pressed needles into his skin. Shooting pain eventually ended with numbness of his extremities. He couldn't feel his legs at all. Using his upper body strength he pulled the side of the eighteen-foot vessel down, bringing it closer to the water. The railing lay over, inches from the water, as if it were expecting him. He threw himself into the open boat and lay there.

Alonzo urged his body to move. He let the mooring-warp loose, set the oars in the locks, and began rowing. His muscles quivered and jerked as he aimed the skiff toward the shore. Wind and tide helped move the dory as he mechanically pulled on the oars. His intensity began to ebb, but he pulled with determination.

At six pm on the sixteenth of October 1938, the dory grounded itself against land, spilling Alonzo onto the wet sand at the tip of the peninsula known as Cape Cod. He abandoned the dory to drift as the tide and wind directed. It would eventually find a beach, be rescued, and returned to its owner, a fisherman named Davy Souza.

Alonzo stumbled across the sand flats as he made his way to higher ground. Lethargy set in, his strength fading. Willpower propelled him. A biting east wind brought rain that stung his face and penetrated his soaked clothing, stealing his thoughts. The cold became an anesthetic. His thoughts felt like dreams of people rushing, men shooting, and flashes of gold. *Homem com ouro*, he whispered. His feet scratched the sand and he stumbled. He fell, then crawled, pulling with his hands across the gritty land. Alonzo would not give up, he'd come too far. The *Hail Mary* passed through his lips as he struggled to keep going.

He huddled on the sand to catch his breath and take stock of his surroundings. A large wharf protruded from the center of the village. The pier had boats tied on three sides and was illuminated by one overhead light. Their buoyant frames danced against the black night, rocking with the wind. Alonzo could make out the silhouette of the merchant vessel he'd left. It was lying at anchor just outside the mooring field. The wooden structure was named *Railroad Wharf* on the charts. It stood on hundreds of pilings and was a quarter of a mile long. He noticed smaller piers along the shore, some with shacks on the ends. A number of larger buildings built on wharfs stood out against the inky sky. Lights from the town glowed at his back. The town was hidden behind three-story buildings that hugged the shore. Lights along the main street gave a soft luster to the sky beyond. Not far from where he'd crawled out of the water, a single house facing the bay had lights in the windows. He was drawn to the radiant shine, to warmth, and life.

Weaving his way past dories and stacks of sixty foot-long hickory poles left by Weir fishermen, he knew his energy was oozing from his body like water sifting through sand. Alonzo Rodriques needed to find shelter before death found him. "Mae de Deus, nao mais," he said. He called to the mother of God for he was sure he could no longer pick up his arms or legs. Unable to move forward, he found a lee from the wind in an alley on the side of Manny's Ship Chandlery. A small tarp lying next to the wall provided shelter. He crawled under the canvas and as far as he was concerned - the lights had gone out.

Chapter 1

The sea was rippling and the air held the promise of another storm as the wooden fishing boat made her way across the top of the Middle Bank, nine miles north of Provincetown harbor on a chilly autumn morning. Davy Souza was in the wheelhouse fixing his location on the chart and entering it into a notebook he kept on a shelf. He wrote the date, October 16, 1938, then how much and what kind of fish he caught in each tow. He kept track of weather and water conditions. The barometer was dropping, but the wind was still manageable. He used a compass, his grandfather's watch, and a lead line to keep track of his position. He'd see what the next tow would bring, determined not to turn toward home until they had something to unload. What this tow held would determine if he would stay in this area or head closer to shore in the lee of the Truro hills. Davy didn't like the thought of going in with an empty fish hold. They'd had good luck at this spot the previous week, so he'd make this tow for two hours.

The new Detroit diesel engine was purring below deck as he sat in his wheelhouse chair with thoughts running through his mind. Davy remembered the day two years ago when he brought the boat back to the wharf with his father's body wrapped in a wool blanket.

His father had dropped, slumping over on deck while they were loading boxes with Pollack. Davy had tried to revive the old man, but his dad was gone within minutes. A black wreath was hung from the mast. As expected, the son followed in his father's footsteps, fishing from the same boat, in the same way, and on the same grounds.

When Davy was a child his dad would be gone for months at a time. He fished as crew on the *Rob Roy* from a dory out on the Grand Banks. Davy had tried fishing from the decks of the same one hundred-ten foot schooner during the summer he turned eighteen. The trip was two months long, monotonous, and dangerous. His father bought his own fishing boat, the *Fanny Parnell,* and Davy fished weekends and school vacations with him. His father taught him where to go to catch the best fish, how to build a net from rope, and how to predict the weather using winds, clouds and sea.

He put away the memories of the past and returned to the business of fishing. The young captain moved the lever next to the steering wheel, slowing the engine. He hollered to his crewman, "Jimmy, it's time." Jimmy Reis knew what was expected on a fishing boat. He didn't complain. He did what was asked, and he could cook. When the crewman poked his head out of the foc'sle door, Davy called out, "Haul Back." There was no talking as the two men worked, bending, pulling, and lifting. The net was heavy and the work tedious. It took half an hour to wrestle the wet salty mass into the boat and dump the catch onto the deck. Before picking up any fish, the heavy twine, floats, and bottom chain had to be lifted and pushed back out, over the side, into the deep salty water to begin another tow.

The captain stepped into the wheelhouse, looked at the compass and turned the helm hard to port, away from the net that was moving closer to the side of the boat. He gave the order to "let the lines go," and the net returned to the sea. Next began the heavy work of shoveling and lifting the catch. Using a pitchfork to grab the wet slippery fish they tossed them into the wooden boxes, sorting the cod from the flounder.

When the net was towing, sifting water, searching for fish, the captain bent to the pile alongside his shipmate. He threw the keepers into wooden boxes until heads and tails were overflowing the sides. The captain paused and scanned the horizon as if searching for something. He said, "Hey Jimmy, can I ask you something?" Having grown up speaking and listening to Portuguese he had a hint of a singsong accent in his words.

"You know about the Fishermen's Association planning a big dance, well, I thought maybe I could ask someone to go with me. What do you think I should say?" Davy stood with his legs apart. His hand was on the towing post, feeling the wire that was attached to the net as if he could communicate with what was on the other end.

Jimmy was older by ten years, married with two children. He was reliable and had a good sense of humor. He looked at Davy and said, "So who's the girl?"

Jimmy had tried to get Davy to date one of his cousins, but Davy kept refusing and so he had stopped asking.

Davy wasn't about to confess that he couldn't take his thoughts off Mary Diogo. He'd known the family all his life. Her father ran the ship chandlery where his dad and now he, purchased their supplies. Davy had never taken much notice of Mary, but recently he began looking at her differently. Davy was five years older and she had always been a little girl to him. Now she looked more like a woman, less a young girl and he felt awkward around her. He was self-conscious on land, but confident at sea, just the opposite of most of his friends.

"Ok, so don't tell me who she is," Jimmy said. "But if I wasn't married and wanted to ask someone out, I'd just come out and ask. She ain't gonna bite. And the worse that can happen," Jimmy paused as the boat rolled, "is she says no. Then that will be that and you can get back to fishing." Jimmy chuckled out loud. The *Fanny Parnell* dipped first to one side and then the other, yawing in her course, pivoting down the sea. The mast dipped twenty degrees to port then twenty to starboard as the narrow boat steered her course.

The wind was picking up, beginning to hum in the rigging as the two men worked side by side for over an hour. "Not bad, ten boxes already and not yet ten in the morning," Davy said. "If this keeps up we'll have a good day's catch." There was constant motion and movement. The fish were gutted, rinsed with salt water, and then stacked on both sides of the boat below deck, the weight evenly distributed. It was back breaking work but both men loved it. "You know what they say Jimmy? East is least, west is best."

The young captain gazed across the water. "The wind is picking up from the east, going to get a bit snotty. We'll give it one shot under the lee of the land before we head in." The captain continued, "I've been thinking of going for Whiting next month. If we get into fish we'll be handling twenty boxes in a tow." The words hung in the air like a gull on the wind. "The price is cheap, but we can make up the difference with weight. We'll need to hire another hand. Do you know anyone looking to crew?"

Jimmy shook his head, "When the time comes we'll find someone." He looked at the gray sky and said, "How long will this tow be? I thought I'd make us something to eat."

Davy answered, "Won't be long. I'll give you a call when we're ready."

Jimmy stood on the deck scanning the horizon instead of heading to the fo'c'sle. He gripped the stay-wire and then stepped into the tiny wheelhouse after the captain. Jimmy's frame took up the entire doorway. Davy smiled at him. His crewman had arms as big as some men's thighs. His biceps were like iron bands and he could lift 150 pounds over his head. He was bowlegged, most likely from rickets when he was a kid. There was a story around town that he and another fellow were seen one day carrying a pole, bigger than a telephone pole, one man lifting each end, all the way from the end of the wharf to the railroad station outside the center of town. The lanky crewman liked to pass the time talking. "I saw Frank Souza the other day. He's your grandfather's cousin. Well, you know he fishes the weir off Truro." Jimmy waited and Davy nodded.

The crewman continued, "Did you know that it takes seventy hickory poles, each one is over sixty feet long, to make one fish weir? Well," Jimmy paused to gather the words, "your grandfather's cousin said they caught a few tuna last month and they were fishtailing it around, inside the big net pen."

Davy knew he was in for a story when Jimmy smiled out of one side of his face. "Well, those fish were slowly swimming round and round. Frank got the harpoon and connected with one weighing close to a thousand pounds. Six men pulled the weir nets closer to the dory, hand over hand." Jimmy's voice was beginning to shake with excitement.

"The crew pulled in the line connecting the harpoon to the fish. When the fish was next to the boat, young Peter O'Mallery — he was new to the crew — well, he stuck a gaff with a big hook on it down its mouth, tugged, hooked it good." Jimmy paused for effect. "My guess is he was thinking he'd get another line on it and help bring it in." Davy waited. Jimmy laughed out loud.

"Well that fish wasn't done. When that hook set the big tuna jumped in the air and pulled the kid up and over the side, gaff and all, quick as a wink, in the drink." Jimmy was laughing so hard he had to stop talking.

"What happened?" Davy asked.

"Well, Frank put another gaff in the boy's belt, hollering to the new hand, '*Let go of the fish, I have a line on your belt, I've got you.*' The kid finally did. They pulled the boy in instead of the tuna. Damn near drown right there in the fish trap. I guess he thought he was going to land that fish all by himself."

Shaking his head he added, "You have to admire the kid, he was soaking wet, but didn't complain. Captain Frank shot the tuna with a double barrel shotgun that he keeps under the tarp in the bow."

Jimmy rolled his shoulders and continued the story. "The silly kid was so embarrassed he went and joined the Army. What with all the unrest in Europe and Asia that might be a little risky right now, but I guess fishing wasn't his cup of tea." Jimmy headed for the foc'sle to make something for them to eat. The captain went back to staring out the wheelhouse window, daydreaming of Mary Diogo.

There is only one chair in the wheelhouse, for the captain, and many hours passed with Davy sitting in it. He watched the compass, the sky, the waves, and the wires that held the net connected to the boat. Heading toward land and the lee of the Truro hills, the fishing boat surged into the sea, rolling and swaying, in that easy familiar way.

The captain thought of the girl he had known all his life, and marveled at the way she seemed to have suddenly grown up before his eyes. He had watched Mary at church on Sunday with the light from the big stained glass windows streaming into the open space causing Mary's hair to glow. He berated himself for having impure thoughts, but couldn't stop imagining running his fingers through her long dark hair, looking into her eyes, kissing her mouth, and tasting her skin. The erotic feelings of passion were there, just below the surface. His desire for her was growing. A sudden pull from the ocean floor caused ropes and wires to fetch, jolting the wooden craft, slowing the forward motion, taking all thoughts of Mary Diogo from Davy's mind. Jimmy was on deck in moments, "What was that, Cap?"

"No telling, not knowing. Let's haul back and see what we got." Davy knew that big rocks lay across the bottom, but he thought he was far enough away from the pile he'd marked on his chart. He started up the one horse, make-n'-break donkey engine that would raise the two boards, or doors, that kept the mouth of the net open. A line ran through a double block and tackle at the top of the mast brought the net up, over the rail. It could be tricky to bring the net safely aboard in rough seas. Davy steered the *Fanny Parnell* maneuvering slowly ahead as he circled the area where his net would rise from the depths.

When Jimmy gave a nod and a holler that the net was clear, Davy put the boat in gear, moving away from the net. He watched the current, the tips of the waves, and the way the boat moved. To pull it under the belly of the boat and into the propeller could be dangerous. They would have to cut the net free to clear any entanglement. He used both the currents and the diesel engine. Once the doors were lashed to the gallows, the men hauled the net closer to the vessel. When the captain thought the net was clear, the *Fanny Parnell* made a circle in the ocean. The two men worked well together. Davy handled the line that ran through the block as Jimmy guided the net onto the deck.

"Grab the splitting strap. We'll bring it up in sections. Let's see what we got."

He wrapped the hemp line around the winch, the brass now curved, shining, and smooth from years of friction. There was enough power between the net and the engine to pull the boat over on its side if conditions were right, if he were careless or if something went wrong. Davy could feel the tension on the wire as it tightened and the vessel leaned into the sea, the net straining and pulling against the forward motion. "Ease off," Davy yelled, "Hold it there. We'll take another loop around the net, then drop what we've got into the deck, bring it in a bit at a time."

They worked together silently until the strain on the gear let go. The net popped, as if a spring had sprung, bouncing to the surface, lying stretched out on the top of the water looking like the rounded back of a whale. Alive with fish pushing against the net, expanding the twine, the full net collided with the surface of the sea, causing the water to churn and swirl. There was a sound of applause, like hundreds of small hands clapping. Slapping wet fins could be heard above the wind. And then Davy let out a whoop of a call, a holler that sounded above the noise of the engine and waves: a shout of joy. "Whoooooeee! We've got a pop-up."

Jimmy laughed along with the captain. "Must be your lucky day," shouted the crewman as he watched the net floating on the surface. "And it looks like we've got our work cut out for us." The fish would have to be cut and gutted. "Good thing we ate breakfast. I'll get the gutting knife and a sharpening stone." Jimmy said.

The sky was darkening, brooding and ominous, collecting steel colored clouds. The water mirrored the sky as if the boat floated inside a cocoon of grey with a vanishing horizon. The line between where the sky began and the sea ended had all but disappeared.

The captain reached for the brailer, a homemade rig used by the weir fishermen to haul fish into their dory-boats, straining out the water. It looked like a butterfly net that could dip fifty or more pounds in one scoop. "Let's lighten the load in the net before we try to bring it aboard. We'll tie the net alongside and dip out all we can and then we'll split the net as it comes up." They worked well together, managing the large load, bringing the net closer to the boat in sections. Davy knew to use the up and down, rocking motion of the water to his advantage, so that as the boat rolled he pulled up the slack line. Feeling his vessel leaning into the sea, he balanced himself and his boat with ease.

The wind had picked up forming curling waves and a five-foot trough, causing the *Fanny Parnell* to yaw as they made their way back to Provincetown Harbor. A cloud of sea gulls followed their wake, knowing that scraps would appear. The rain came as the boat rounded Long Point. Their work would be complete when the boat was tied up for the night, but they still had hundreds of pounds of fish on deck, all needing to be cleaned. It would take hours. Jimmy stepped into the doorway of the wheelhouse and pointed toward the stern, out into the night. "Looks like a freighter took refuge from the storm. We made it in just in time." Jimmy gave the captain a nod.

Davy took the boat out of gear. It glided across the harbor as Davy strained to see into the rain washed night toward the waiting wharf. "I don't see the dory. We did leave it on the mooring this morning, didn't we?" Jimmy scratched his head and looked to the spot where their eighteen-foot skiff was supposed to be tied. It wasn't there.

The captain was shaking his head. "We'll leave the boat on the wharf tonight after we unload. I'm sure it will be okay."

They cleaned the rest of the catch standing at the railing in black-oiled hats, overcoats, and boots that protected them from the October rain. They cut the throats of the fish, pulling the innards out with one swipe, and feeding them to the fish and fowl. The cod were large. Many weighed over ten pounds each. Davy estimated the haul at 5,000 pounds, a catch to be proud of. They would unload the fish at Fishermen's Wharf. The large pier held an ice plant, cold storage building, and unloading platform. Davy had a choice of six different icehouses, but preferred this one because it was close to the town center, just west of Railroad Wharf and he thought the prices he was paid were fair. At the end of each trip, three or four times a week, a variety of fish in varying amounts left Provincetown heading by truck or train to Boston, New Bedford and New York. Some days, like today, thousands of pounds, other days — nothing. During extreme winter weather boats would tie up and the fishermen stayed home.

Water was dripping from the brims of their sou'westers when they finished. Jimmy said, "I'd say we were the high-liners today, quite a haul."

The captain replied, "Yea, but I don't like that our skiff *Little Fanny* is gone. I thought we had a good mooring and I know you tied it right." Jimmy nodded. Nothing like this had ever happened to him before, but they both knew that boats broke away from moorings for a variety of reasons: wear and tear on the lines or a shackle lets go. Theft was not considered.

"We'll look for the skiff in the morning," Davy said. "If we're lucky we'll find it somewhere on the west end. With the wind from the east that's where it'll wind up." It had been a good day and Captain Davy was not going to let the missing dory ruin it. "With this weather it doesn't look like we'll get out tomorrow. There's a meeting of the fishermen's association I'd like to go to. That big dance is going to raise money for the Red Cross and the Ladies Aid Society."

"I heard a little about it, sounds like a good idea. Stop by and get me in the morning, I'll help you look for the dory," his crewman said. They shook hands, as was their habit.

Davy turned right onto a darkened Commercial Street. Seamen's Bank on the corner of Ryder Street was closed, as was the Men's Shop, Louis's New York Store, and most of the businesses. Johnny Mott's pool hall, the Pilgrim House and the Colonial Tap were still open. It was past nine o'clock and he'd been up for eighteen hours. His body was weary, but his thoughts were energized as he wondered how to ask Mary out. He was talking out loud to himself, a habit he'd developed from being alone on the boat all day. "I'll drop in at the Ship Chandlery tomorrow and bring Manny Diogo a fish. I could use new gloves, some mending twine, and a couple of new needles." He would ask about the family. Maybe she would be there. His words were heard only by the rain and wind.

The young captain could feel his anticipation growing, anxiety mixed with excitement. He thought about Mary. He pushed his hands into his pockets, bent his head, his eyes searched the ground as if he might find the right words written there. He rounded the corner at Pearl Street and because he wasn't looking, bumped into a man. Through the rain their eyes met briefly with no sign of recognition. Both grunted what sounded like an apology. Davy watched the reflection in the glass windows of the shop as the stranger walked in the opposite direction. He was wearing a fine-tailored winter coat and felt hat pulled down low on his head. He was not a fisherman or anyone else he recognized from town. Davy thought no more about the incident because his thoughts were elsewhere. First he would ask Mary to go out with him to see a movie. *The Adventures of Robin Hood* was playing at the Pilgrim Theater. If that went well, maybe she would go with him to the big dance. He whistled softy as he walked the last few feet to his home. Even the cold rain couldn't dampen his spirits.

Chapter 2

The storm that left Alonzo on the beach and drove the *Fanny Parnell* back to Provincetown Harbor caused Manny Diogo to lock the front door of his ship chandlery earlier than usual and head to the warm kitchen where his wife Eleanor was looking at a newspaper. She raised her head. "President Roosevelt says he's going to keep us out of war." Eleanor reached out her hand to her husband, "Seems the world is full of unrest, mirror's this stormy weather." Manny kissed her neck, surprising her, making her laugh.

"I've got some good news for you." Manny said. "James Crawley came into the shop today." The three had grown up living within a few blocks of each other. When Manny married Eleanor, James went away to college, the Army, and then the police academy. After working in Boston for a number of years, he came back to his hometown as Police Chief. Their friendship remained, but their lives intercepted less frequently. Manny had been surprised by the chief's visit. It was not like in the old days when they had few responsibilities and more time.

Eleanor asked, "And how is dear James? Why didn't you bring him back for tea?" She felt a kindness and gentleness toward their childhood friend. It was a feeling that she couldn't explain to anyone. Eleanor loved her husband and so it was an emotion never explored or spoken of. "What did he want? I hope it wasn't police business."

Manny squared his shoulders, sucking in breath, feeling a quiver of excitement pass through him. "James is fine, sends his love. Said he couldn't stay but a minute. I'll tell you the news at supper with the girls." Eleanor waited for more, so he added, "No, no. It's nothing to do with police business. You don't need to worry." He sat down in his usual chair.

Seeing first the positive and the good in all things, Eleanor looked at the glass as half-full. Manny called her a Pollyanna, but she sounded worried tonight as she continued, "This war business has me jumpy. And this storm reminds me of the hurricane last month, so much sadness," she said. She handed him the paper. "I was reading about the Neutrality Act that Congress has passed. Sounds like the President is trying to ease our worries. Just the same, the idea of war makes my heart ache." She didn't sound her usual upbeat self. She was worrying and couldn't express her thoughts, as if something was about to happen, something like the hurricane that she was not prepared for. She placed her hands on her husband's shoulders and continued, "But there are good things happening as well. I read in the paper that a time capsule will be buried on the grounds of the 1939 World's Fair in New York City and it won't be opened until the year 6939. Imagine that. I'll bet the girls will get a kick out of that bit of news."

"That's too far away for me," he said. "The news last night was that the House of Representatives has authorized a special committee to investigate un-American activities. They're going to call it the Federal Bureau of Investigation. I suspect the government didn't know what to do with all the G-men when the Volstead Act was repealed, now that alcohol can be bought anywhere." Manny kept up with the news each night, reading aloud to his wife and sometimes repeating stories to his daughters. Mary his oldest at seventeen would understand what was happening in the world, but Emily and Juliana he protected from the harsh realities of the world news. He read the newspaper funnies to the girls on Sunday morning. He didn't talk to his younger daughters about the tension and turbulence growing in the country. People had marched in protests in Boston and New York, demanding better working conditions, more than one day off a week, and increased pay.

"The country is restless and changing, like a lobster growing out of its shell." Manny said. He spoke to his three girls about the fishermen forming an association, taking their cause all the way to the Boston State House. What was not spoken of at the dinner table was the news of strikes and unions forming across America, the war in Spain, or the political upheaval in

Europe. Although the hurricane was spoken of, the horrific lose of life on September 21 was not. Their small family had no concept of the destruction and death that was already happening on the other side of the world. When death came to their town it was brought by disease, by old age, or from the sea. The destruction in other parts of the globe had not touched the sandy shores of Cape Cod. The concept of war was almost nonexistent. The fishing people at the end of the peninsula lived in a world separate, apart, and at peace.

"What I'd like to know is how long till supper? I'm starved." The routine was the same most days, so he didn't wait for a reply. Smiling, she returned to her cooking. Manny called over his shoulder, "I'll be in the office. Call me when supper is ready." She had every night for eighteen years.

Reaching for a piece of wood that was kept in the box next to the cast iron cooker Eleanor glanced out her rain-splattered window. Something caused her to pause. A shape seemed to be moving against the exposed sand that stretched for half a mile with Railroad Wharf looming in the distance. Narrowing her brows and leaning into the pane of glass, she rubbed the window with her towel and squinted into the twilight. Eleanor was watching something out of the ordinary. A black smudge contrasting against the tan colored sand was moving. There was no one there to hear her say, "What is that?" She opened the door that led to the hall and the office. "Manuel, can you come take a look at this? I saw something beyond our wharf, out on the flats," she called.

Manny was bent over the ledger books. He looked up and answered, "I'll be right there." He came up behind his petite wife as she turned back to the window.

"Over there." She touched the windowpane. He pressed his front to her back, fitting himself around her as she wiped the steam away with the rag.

Manny spoke softly, "It's dark, I can't see much with this rain, but I don't see anything unusual." He paused scanning the harbor taking in the sand flats and shoreline, "Nothing is moving that shouldn't be." In the next breath he whispered, "Except me." He cleared his throat and his voice became serious, "Want me to go out and take a look?"

Eleanor drew her eyebrows together, scrutinizing the area beyond her window, waiting for the phantom to appear, for something to move. She shook her head, looking at the empty area. "Must be this rain making things move that shouldn't be." She patted her husband's back as she kissed his cheek. Feeling a chill, she reached for a piece of wood and dropped it into the stove.

Manny reassured her, "It was most likely a fisherman heading home in the rain."

25

Eleanor called the girls for their evening meal: fried cod, potatoes and homemade bread. The fish was a gift from Captain Joseph Macara of the *Annabelle R.* who had stopped at Manny's Ship Chandlery. The fisherman had picked up turnbuckles and a spool of twine, leaving the fish as a gift. Mary, Emily, and Juliana brought their jubilations and chatter into the kitchen, taking away all thoughts of strange apparitions.

Manny tucked the newspaper behind him. "I hear the fishermen are going to be holding a big dance at the Town Hall." All talk stopped. "The Provincetown Fishermen's Association has invited some of the townspeople and the business community to a get together to plan a fundraiser and celebration. I've been asked to join them." The kitchen stove sizzled and snapped as everyone sat listening.

"We've all heard about the big storm last month. Provincetown lost some property, trees, and a few boats were destroyed, but the town was spared the worst of it." Manny had debated bringing up the awful destruction, but he felt that even the youngest daughter should have some knowledge of what Mother Nature could do. "That hurricane hit hard to the south and west of us, over fifty thousand homes and businesses were destroyed." He didn't tell his daughters of the six hundred and fifty people who had lost their lives.

The girls stopped speaking, forks and knives suspended, remembering the storm as if digesting the news instead of the food. Their father continued, "Remember how our basement flooded and how the sand filled in the alley. We were cleaning up for days." He let this sink in, "We lost some supplies, but the bulkhead stayed strong and things quickly returned to normal. Well, not so in other places."

The girls looked at their father with genuine interest. "Our problems here are nothing compared to what happened along the Connecticut and Rhode Island shoreline," he said. The news reports in the paper and on the radio were of complete devastation. Manny enjoyed his daughters' laughter and preferred to spotlight the good in life, but he also knew that a dose of reality was a good thing for even his youngest daughter, Juliana who had celebrated her tenth birthday this month. "Well, the good news is that Chief Crowley came by the shop today and said he'd been asked if he could recommend someone in the business community to help out in raising money for the victims of the hurricane. I've been asked to come to a meeting of the Provincetown Fishermen's Association to help plan what they are calling the Provincetown Fishermen's Association's First Anniversary Ball." His enthusiasm was infectious. He had a grin from ear to ear. The girls giggled in response. He had everyone's attention when he said,

"It's a way for us to celebrate, give thanks to our maker, and to raise money for the communities that were hardest hit by the big storm." He looked at Eleanor and saw a smile pulling her rosy cheeks up, into an expression of delight.

"So that's the surprise. That sounds wonderful." Eleanor looked around the table.

All three girls began asking questions. Their voices a mix of wonder and surprise, "Can I go?" "When is it?" "Will you get a new dress, mama?" "Can I go?" They laughed as they wiggled in their seats, dancing to an unheard rhythm. Their voices formed a din of questions.

Manny stopped the chatter, "I don't know what the men will decide. We are getting together on Friday: fishermen, businesses, and townsmen. But, I think that maybe this dance is for adults only." Manny thought this would stop the chatter, but he was wrong. An explosion of words and sighs reverberated through the small kitchen. He put his hands in the air, palms out, and raised his voice, "It's just in the planning stages and it's not my decision." The room grew quiet. "The fishermen came up with the idea and now the community is going to help put it together. That's all I know."

Manny thought about the fishermen who came into his shop, captains and crewmen who worked the boats that supported his business. Good men, strong of spirit with hands like leather. He respected these hard-working men and always stopped to talk with them when they came to his chandlery. He kept a ledger and file cards with their names and orders: Louis Salvador, Joe Lisbon, Manuel Macara John Russe, Edmund Gill, Jack Joseph, Frank Parsons, Henry Passion, Victor Reis, David Souza, Ramires Malaquias, Norbert Macara, Tony Thomas, and so many others that he saw less frequently. Manny had tried his hand at fishing, but wasn't good at it. He got seasick and he never seemed to be able to sleep. That was before he'd married, inherited the building from Eleanor's family, and opened the marine store.

"It's a dance to celebrate with the fishing community," Manny said. "Its in January, after the holidays. We can go if you'd like, Eleanor." He sat up taller and beamed.

Eleanor smiled at him and turned to her daughters' expectant faces. She stood up. Laughing, she began moving her feet in a four-part square. She lifted her skirt to her knees and sang a tune in 4/4 time. One she'd heard as a child, "La, la, la, la, la by Strauss, by Strauss." Everyone laughed at her antics. "Ah, to dance the evening away in the arms of my husband." Eleanor looked at Manny. "The last time we danced together was on our wedding day, eighteen years ago. Remember Manny?" She smiled again, knowing that he did not like dancing. He loved holding her in his arms and maybe with a little coaxing he would dance with her again.

Mary piped up, "Mom, we do the boogie-woogie today. I don't think anyone dances the waltz anymore." All three daughters joined in the laughter and got up to show their parents how it was done.

"That's enough. I don't believe the dance will be this boogie-woogie music you're talking about." The girls stopped jumping around when their father continued, "The dance is for adults and we dance the foxtrot and waltz."

The three young ladies looked at their mother with disbelief. Eleanor said, "Just remember, you will all have the opportunity for dancing when you are older." Three frowning faces looked back at their mother. That ended the conversation, but not the grumbling sound that came from the three girls.

Manny rose from the table, "Tides still out, rain seems to be letting up. I think I'll take a walk and check the mooring block for the dory." He was donning his coat and slipping into his boots before his wife could say anything. He heard the disappointment in his daughters' voices, not the giggles that usually followed supper as he closed the kitchen door. Dampness saturated the air in swirling clouds of vapor. His breath joined the mist as he stepped outside. Still thinking of the clam digger, he walked in the direction where Eleanor had pointed. The shopkeeper made his way down the steps to the beach, heading west toward Railroad Wharf in the center of town, observing no set path between moorings, rocks and pilings that the low tide had uncovered. Keeping alert, he skirted the shoreline. The storm was passing, the wind abating, leaving the clean scent of washed seaweed. In a few hours the water would cover the beach where he was standing.

He sometimes talked to himself, sure that no one could hear, mumbling as he glanced beyond the sand to the large open bay. He could see his breath illuminated against the dark sky. "Most likely Eleanor's wild imagination, seeing things, or an old fisherman. There is nothing moving out here now." Even with a misty rain obscuring his vision he could see the shadows of a few boats swinging gently on their moorings in deeper water. Everything was as it should be. He felt a cold wind cross his exposed skin. He turned, quickened his pace, and returned to the warmth of his home.

The next day dawned bright and clear. The storm had left fresh air, uplifted spirits and a chilly north wind. Eleanor had been up for hours. Manny was in the shop and the three girls were off to school with books and lunches. On days such as this one, laundry hangs on a line stretched between two poles on a patch of ground outside the kitchen door. Their living area on the water was both a worry and a blessing. Storms at high tide had flooded the basement on a few occasions and the wooden bulkhead was a source of concern. But because of the beauty in their yard, their home on the water was a continual source of delight.

The Diogo family used this door leading to the beach for personal use. It was where their children met friends, playing on the sand flats in warmer weather. There is a patch of ground no larger than their bedroom that had a small wharf attached. The small pier protruded into the water and was used to load heavier supplies directly onto the boats at high tide. This morning Eleanor made her way to the clothesline on that small piece of earth and set the basket down on the rain-washed ground.

The fresh smell of cleansed dirt and tumbled sea caused her to breath deeply as she reached for the clothing. When she stretched to place a girls dress on the line she heard a soft thumping sound coming from the marine room under the house. Manny stored supplies on the level below her. Someone might be looking for her husband. She called "hello?" No voice returned, but the muffled noise came again. She called a second time, and waited. When the sound came again she placed the dress back in the basket. Moving quickly, she went down the stairs. Her feet touched the ground and she turned into the alley on the east side of the house expecting an unlatched door. She was surprised to see a mound of canvas in the corner near the entrance to their marine room. Eleanor studied the shape. Then it moved, and she jumped. "Manny, come quick I need you," she yelled.

Eleanor lifted the tarp with caution. A man lay beneath it. She ran up the alley to the front door of the shop and found her husband talking with Davy Souza. They looked at her with surprise as she shouted at them, "There's a man here that needs help. I think he's unconscious." She didn't need to say more. The men followed Eleanor into the alley.

Manny rolled the man over. "Well, he's still breathing." He looked at his wife, "Eleanor call Doc Rice. Clear off the cot in the office, and then come and hold the door for us." He turned to Captain Souza. "He's in some sort of shock and soaking wet. We need to get him warm right away." Eleanor hurried up the stairs. Manny spoke with a firm voice, "Can you hear me? We're going to help you. You're going to be fine." He had no idea if this were true or if the man could even hear him. The shopkeeper knew many people in town, but he didn't recognize this one. His black hair was hanging like seaweed, and a dark shadow of a beard concealed half his face. His clothes were made of wool and were heavy with water. "Do you know him?" Manny asked the fisherman as the two men knelt close to the man.

"No. I don't think I've seen him before," Davy said. The stranger lay unmoving, but then his eyes fluttered and he spoke. The words were garbled, not complete. The two Provincetown men looked at each other, shaking their heads, neither rescuer understood, even though each had heard Portuguese spoken before.

The shopkeeper said, "Let's get him upstairs. Can you take him under his arms?" The young captain nodded. The two men rolled him onto his back. Davy hooked his arms under the strangers armpits. Manny grabbed the man's legs and together they carried him up the stairs. The wood stove was burning low in the kitchen as they passed. They turned left into the office and gently placed the man on the cot. The small office was crowded.

Manny looked at his wife. "Eleanor, there are long johns and blankets in the shop, you know where they are." She nodded and left. Davy moved into the hall to wait. Eleanor hurried from the shop carrying a bundle. Manny spoke to her quietly, almost in a whisper. "Did you call the doctor?" She nodded yes.

He continued, "Help me get him out of his wet clothes." They removed his coat, then pulled the sweater, pants, and long underwear from the man's body. The last layer of flannel was brown and worn with age, wet and clinging.

When she touched his skin Eleanor was reminded of yesterday's fish, firm, cold and clammy. They bundled him into new flannel underwear, wrapped a woolen blanket around him, and place a quilt over the top of the bed. They spoke in whispers as if in church. The man seemed barely alive.

When Manny left the office he found Davy waiting in the hallway. The shopkeeper said, "Ask around the wharf, find out if anyone is missing a crewman. He's dressed like a seaman, don't you think?" Davy said he looked like a fisherman. Manny continued, "Someone will be looking for him. In the meantime we'll wait for the doc." Davy followed Manny into the shop.

Eleanor stayed in the office. She hung the stranger's coat on a hanger in the closet and then pulled the swivel chair from under Manny's desk. She sat watching the stranger while waiting for the doctor to arrive, wondering why this man was in such a state. She thought his family would be worried when he didn't return. And that caused her to think about her own family. This stranger appeared to be near the same age as her daughter Mary who would be eighteen, graduating high school in June and would then attend the Women's College in Hyannis next September.

Her three girls were growing up. Fourteen year-old Emily was constantly on the move, dancing up and down the stairs to music from the radio, especially Benny Goodman and his band. She practiced the violin and it drove her sisters from their shared room, but they all loved to hear the swinging, swaying sounds of Sammy Kaye or Tommy Dorsey. Emily was quick and had an answer for everything. She said what was on her mind. She did not know fear and did not spend time worrying. The innocence of youth was holding her hand while the physical world pulled her into the future.

The youngest sister, Juliana was ten. She was either following her father around like a puppy or pestering her older sisters. Juliana had the face of an angel and could pout like the devil when refused her way, but everyone doted on her. Eleanor was roused from her daydream by the moaning of the man on the cot. She placed her hand on his head and felt a transferring of warmth from her palm onto his pale skin. He was so cold. She moved her hand and tucked the blanket around his shoulders.

Pulling the chair closer to the cot, she leaned over, and said, "You are safe now. You are going be okay. Can you hear me?" He lay still, not responding. He had shaggy dark hair, black stubble on his face, and long dark eyelashes. When she helped to change his clothing she noticed the muscular upper body, but his ribs could be seen as if he'd not eaten well for some time. His hands were callused, hard, and leathery, most certainly from hard work in all kinds weather.

He was a stranger to her, but many boats tied to the various wharfs around town and she did not know everyone. People came and went daily. She watched boats moving around the waterfront from her kitchen window. If he was not from the Provincetown fleet then it might take days or weeks to contact his family. She could not think about that now. First he needed to get well. Eleanor was glad to hear voices in the hall. The doctor had arrived.

Chapter 3

Everyone in town knew Doctor Rice. He delivered babies, helped the sick or injured, and sat with the dying. Manny was in the store behind the counter talking with Davy Souza when the doctor arrived. The local fisherman was saying, "I was on the wharf earlier this morning, but I didn't hear of anyone missing. I'll ask around." He tipped his hat to the doctor as he left the shop.

Manny shook the doctor's hand, "Thanks for coming. Your patient is in the office." He put the "closed" sign in the front door. Doc Rice followed him down the hall to the office. "We found him in the alley soaking wet and called as soon as we could," Manny said.

Eleanor opened the office door for the two men. "He hasn't said anything. We changed him into dry clothing." She waited but the doctor only nodded. She continued, "I'll wait in the kitchen. Let me know if I can help." Looking out the window she could see that the tide was high, filling the large harbor. The water was just below the top of the bulkhead with sun sparkling on its surface. A small flame in the cook stove was warming the room and it reminded her that she needed to bring in wood to keep the bread rising. The cook stove provided warmth for daytime living. There was a parlor stove upstairs that was lit during the evening on cold nights.

Eleanor felt uncomfortable, excited, and anxious. There was turmoil and confusion in her home, a rare thing. She glanced out the window again. The basket under the clothesline was a reminder that her life would have to wait. Time slowed, shrinking in, not quite standing still, but easing, allowing her a quiet moment. She sighed.

Fifteen minutes later Dr. Rice came into the kitchen. Taking a deep breath he said, "Eleanor, his body temperature is a bit low. We need to warm him up, but at the same time, watch for fever. We don't want to over heat him." She nodded her understanding. "You've done the right thing getting him out of the wet clothing." The doctor made notes on a pad he'd taken from his pocket. "I need you to keep a close eye on him while I make some arrangements for him to be taken to the hospital. If he wakes, I mean wide awake, and talking, give him warm liquids, but only if he is awake."

Eleanor pulled her sweater closer, tucking her arms under each other as if hugging her tiny frame. The doctor continued, "His lungs are clear, no sign of fever or rash, that's good." The big man put his hand on her shoulder. "I'll have to find someone to drive the ambulance to Hyannis." He picked up his black bag as he said, "I'll come back after I check in at the office. The hospital can deal with him if he doesn't wake up, but I've a feeling he'll be awake soon." Eleanor was remembering how the doctor's gentle hands had delivered all three of her daughters. She caught herself daydreaming when the doctor said, "Meanwhile, keep an eye on him."

She thanked him as they walked to the shop. Eleanor told Doc Rice that they would trade him a barrel of tar or a nice shackle for his services. He laughed. "My fee will come from that young man. He looks fit, and strong enough to pay his own way." Then the older man leaned close to Eleanor and lowered his voice, "I'll be back as soon as I can. Call me if you have a problem. And keep the girls out of the room. We don't really know what's happened to him. I don't think he's contagious. It looks like hypothermia, but we won't take any chances. Let's see how this develops." The doctor went into the shop to speak with Manny.

Eleanor stood on the threshold of the office after the doctor left. Her patient appeared to be asleep. The color in his cheeks was returning, less grey, more olive. She thought he looked handsome, with strong cheekbones, a Phoenician nose, and thick hair. "Who knows what you've been up to?" Eleanor was thinking out loud as she closed the door. It was a mystery to her as to how he'd arrived at their doorstep. Travel by water brought boats to their harbor all year long, at all hours of the day and night. Fishing boats, ferry boats and yachts of all sizes came distances to stop for refuge against the sandy shores. People also came to town by train, but only the wealthy could afford the new automobiles. She had heard that they cost as much as a house.

Eleanor spent the next few hours going back and forth between kitchen and her husband's office. She kept a pitcher of water and a basin on the desk that she used to bath his face and hands. He opened his eyes a number of times, staring as if he were looking through her, not at her. He watched her, but did not protest her motherly ministering.

Later that day Dr. Rice returned and was greeted by an excited Eleanor. "He's awake. He took a few sips of water."

"I'll take a look at him and talk to you in a few minutes." The doctor closed the door. Eleanor headed to the kitchen. Manny remained in the shop. When Doctor Rice returned carrying his black bag he had a smile on his face. "He's going to live, must be your good nursing care." He looked out the kitchen window without speaking. He seemed to be enjoying the view. After a moment he said, "Eleanor, do you think you and Manny could keep him here for a couple of days? There's no need to send him to the hospital. What he needs is rest, good food, and a little medicine." He didn't want to tell her that Clem Silva had said the ambulance was in the shop getting new brakes and that they would have to use one of the fish trucks to take the man to Hyannis. "I don't believe he's in any kind of danger. This is not what I'd call an emergency situation."

Eleanor didn't hesitate. "Yes, of course he can stay. I'll speak to Manny, but I'm sure he will agree." It was decided before anyone had time to change his or her minds.

The doctor mentioned that their patient spoke Portuguese and very little English. "He'll be on his feet in a couple of days," he said as he left. "I'll stop in tomorrow, call if you need me. Mrs. Cabral is about to have her second child and there's a case of mumps up the west end. My office will find me."

Later that day as the sun was setting over Provincetown Harbor, husband and wife discussed how they would tell their daughters about the guest in the office. Mary, Emily and Juliana were called to the table for their evening meal. When everyone was settled, Manny stood up and said, "Girls, I need your attention." His daughters were bright and eager as they waited for their father's announcement. "This morning your mother found a man outside, near the marine room. He's ill and he needs to rest. He'll be staying with us for a few days." The three daughters had questions, but their father raised his hand to stop them. "He is in my office on the cot. I need to ask you to be respectful and quiet." The young women were all eyes and ears as their father continued, "Just help your mother. And please stay out of the office, doctor's orders."

He cleared his throat. The girls sat in silence and then, like an explosion, each girl had questions. "Who is he? Can I see him? Where did he come from? Mother found him? What was he doing? What does he look like? Is he someone we know?" It was a cornucopia of young female voices, usually a melody to their father's ears, but tonight – an increasing ruckus. Eleanor clapped her hands together. "Quiet down. Right now he needs rest. You'll find out everything about him in good time. Now finish eating, clear the table, and then upstairs. Whose turn is it to wash?" The girls knew the routine. Dad went upstairs carrying the paper and an armful of split wood to make an evening fire in the Franklin stove. It would be a chilly night.

The girls moved around in the small kitchen, occasionally brushing up against each other, giggling to each other over the news of the stranger. Mary asked, "Mom can you tell us more about the man in the office? What happened to him?" The four females stopped what they were doing when Mary spoke, "How sick is he and is it catching?"

Their mother was gentle, "The doctor doesn't think it's catching. We don't know much about him. I think he may be a fisherman from one of the transient boats. I'll let you know everything as we learn more about him." She looked at each girl to be sure they understood what she was telling them. "Doc Rice said for you to stay out of the room for a couple of days. Understood? Apparently he doesn't speak English, only Portuguese." This stopped the questions.

"Now upstairs all of you, and please take an armful of wood with you. The three young ladies turned to leave. Their mother called after them, "And Mary, help Emily and Juliana with their schoolwork. I'll be up as soon as I can." They each took wood from the stack and headed for the stairs.

Eleanor returned to her husband's office. This was a place that was always organized. Now it looked tossed. Ledger books, stacks of paper on the desk, and boxes of marine items piled on the floor was not how her husband liked to keep the office. She ignored the room and looked at the stranger. He lay unmoving. Sounds were coming from him, not words, but a moan, a murmur, speaking in his sleep. She sat at the desk chair and held her breath, listening to the words, *"Tesouro, traidor"* coming from his lips.

She bent closer and could see his chest rise and fall. His words were faint, but audible, familiar. She silently repeated them, *"Tesoro? Traydor."* The words meant nothing to her. He was having a dream. She had never been this close to another man and felt an unexplainable embarrassment.

He opened his eyes and looked at her. No smile formed on his sensuous mouth, but his eyes softened. *"Obrigado,"* he whispered.

"You're going to be all right sir. Would you like something to eat? Can you hear me?" Her words tentative, her voice hushed. "Food," she said and motioned with her fingers to her mouth.

"Sim, por favor," he murmured. He tried to raise himself. Sweating with the exertion, he slumped back into the pillow.

"You will need to sit up a little, I'll get more pillows." She ran up the flight of stairs and pulled a pillow from their bed. The girls were sitting around the stove with books and papers sprawled across the rug. Sounds of hushed music came from the RCA Victor Radio. Everyone looked up expectantly. "He's awake. I'm going to give him some fish broth," Eleanor said. Her husband asked if she needed help, but she shook her head no.

Back inside the office Eleanor arranged the pillows. She lifted his shoulders and stuffed it down so that his head was high enough to sip the broth and take the two pills that Dr. Rice had left. She could smell the sour odor of perspiration. He looked frail. "Just a boy," she thought. She fed him a few spoonfuls.

He closed his eyes and motioned with his head, "*No mais. Obrigado.*"

Eleanor slipped from the room, ran up the stairs and told her family that their guest had taken the medicine and eaten. Manny replied, "Good, if he's taking nourishment we know he'll live, and he'll soon be on his way." Then he smiled.

Later that night they talked about their unusual day. Eleanor approached the subject cautiously, "Manny, the young man said something to me. It sounded like '*tesouro*' and then '*traidao*.' Like that, in Portuguese." She waited a moment and when no response came she asked, "Do you know what it means?" She had grown up in Provincetown among a large population of Portuguese, but she did not speak the language. Her husband was more familiar.

"The words could mean anything or you may have heard wrong. Maybe he was saying '*trepidar*'. It means trembling or chills. *Tesouro* I believe means treasure." Manny thought for a moment. "He was dreaming of treasures."

Eleanor added, "Doesn't the word *trador* m e a n traitor or treacherous?"

Manny was practical, "People say bizarre things with fever. Don't put much stock in it."

Eleanor smiled at her husband and he said, "Let's get him well and to where he belongs. Then things can get back to normal around here." They were sympathetic to the fellow's plight, but their main concern was for their daughters. "The girls have so many questions and they all want to help." Eleanor said, "One minute everyone is talking about the big dance and the next they are whispering about the stranger." She knew that Mary had already peeked into the office when she thought no one was looking. When caught by her mother, she blushed.

Manny was a realist. "Tell them the truth. We don't know anything about him, and he's not well. And for God's sake, keep them out of the office." He sighed, kissed her cheek and rolled in the bed. "Let's see what tomorrow brings." He slept well. She did not. Laying awake Eleanor thought of the stranger's muddled words, his sweet young face, and of reasons why someone would show up at her door in such a condition.

Eleanor rose before the sun. Wrapped in a warm wool robe, she crept down the stairs to add wood to the kitchen stove that had been burning low throughout the night. When she peeked in to check on their visitor he looked back at her with dark, half-opened eyes. "Oh, I'm glad to see you are awake," she said. "Do you understand?" He nodded. She continued, "I'll bring tea and medicine."

He nodded his head, mumbling words she did not understand. "*Onde uma jaqueta, por favor.*"

She shook her head, unable to understand what he was saying. "I'll bring tea," she said as she left the small office.

Music was playing softly on the radio while she moved around the kitchen. She was humming along with *A-Tisket, A-Tasket* that Ella Fitzgerald was singing. Her husband came into the kitchen. She turned to him, saying, "He doesn't speak much English. He spoke to me in Portuguese, and I didn't understand any of it, except *Obrigado.*"

Manny picked up the cup of coffee that his wife poured for him. "I'll ask Davy Souza to help. I expect I'll see him today in the shop. He has an order to pick up, unless he's gone out fishing. He ordered new gloves and shackles so I expect he'll be around. And Doc Rice will be coming back, but Davy speaks the language much better."

Eleanor placed a pot of tea, cup, sugar and cream on a tray. She put two pills on a napkin and was about to return to her patient when Manny reached out to her. "Have I told you today how much I love you?"

She murmured a sound, without words, kissed his mouth then turned and left.

The house came alive earlier than usual that morning. Mary came downstairs asking her mother if she needed help with breakfast. Eleanor smiled at her oldest and said, "Are your sisters up and moving in the right direction?" Mother and daughter looked at one another and it struck Eleanor that Mary was becoming a beautiful woman.

Mary had her hair tied back, away from her face, looking more than her seventeen years. It was clear from her expression that Mary wanted to remain in the kitchen but she went to help her siblings without a fuss. She found Emily sitting up with her feet on the floor. "Burr, I'm cold. I think I'll wear my wool stocking to school today," Emily said.

"Save your woolies for winter, if you start wearing them now they'll be worn out by the time you really need them. What will you do when it really gets cold?" Mary was clearly in charge. She moved across the room and said, "Come on Miss Julie, it's almost seven. Rise and shine." She added, "Emily, wear your cotton stockings, the day will warm and the stove at school will have you itching if you wear the wool." Before leaving Mary said, "If you want to eat before school you'd better get a move on."

They watched her go. "Well, she's in a hurry. Oh that's right. I'll bet she is going to peek again at you-know-who," Emily laughed.

"What are you talking about?" the younger sister rubber her eyes, yawned and stretched like a cat.

Her sibling said, "Didn't you see the way Mary has been peeking in the office?" The two younger girls hurried into their school clothing. The family ate breakfast and supper at the kitchen table together. Lunches were left over meals, placed in cloth bags, one for each girl to carry to school. They talked of their day ahead, "I have to stay after school today with the orchestra to practice, mom. So I can't walk home with Julie. Mary can do it." Emily said.

"I hope this isn't going to be every day." The older sister replied. "She's really old enough to walk by herself. I was going to spend time with Teresa Perry after school, so we can do homework together." The chatter went back and forth until Eleanor stood up so that the girls knew to listen.

"Mary, for today, pick up your sister at the Center School on your way home, it can't be helped. I'll see what we can do for the rest of the week. I'm sure we can work out a schedule that will satisfy everyone, now off you go."

As Mary headed for the door, she asked, "Mom, how is the man in the office?"

"He's awake, but I haven't had a chance to talk to him yet. You'd better hurry." Each daughter received a kiss and a lunch bag as they left the warm kitchen.

Eleanor put a thick slice of bread in a bowl, added hot milk, brown sugar and cinnamon. The office had no window, but the hall light illuminated the figure on the cot. She stepped into the small area. She turned on the desk lamp because there was no window. "Hello. Good morning. I hope you're feeling better." Her voice was cheerful, but tentative, soft and polite as if she were addressing the church priest.

"*Si, Senhora*," he said, his voice husky from sleep. The fever was gone, but weakness remained. Eleanor felt a surge of pity for the stranger, a maternal need to nurse and care for him. Manny had told her she was the best mother this side of the Atlantic and the most loving of wives. Their marriage had survived the trials that life brought to their doorstep, the death of a child at birth, the care of dying parents, and now a guest they knew nothing about who was suddenly the center of everyone's attention.

"I've brought you something to eat." She placed the tray on her husband's desk. He nodded his head but said nothing. There was something old in his eyes, even though she knew he was in his early twenties. She asked, "Is there someone I can call for you, your family, your mama?"

He shook his head. *"Nao comprendo,"* he said. Then with embarrassment, *"Posso usar o banheiro."* Eleanor froze. He was asking her for the toilet.

Her face reddened, "I'll get my husband." She left the room.

Chapter 4

Manny Diogo arrived at the American Legion Hall for the first of many meetings to plan the Anniversary Ball. The room was filled with smoke, chatter and men. As he made his way to a place along the wall, he stopped to shake hands with fishermen who frequented his shop, asking questions about business and families. There were twenty to thirty men in the room. He recognized many, but there were a few men he'd never seen before. It was quite a turnout.

Charles Forrest and Clarence Santos were standing together at the front of the room, the oldest skipper and the youngest side by side. They turned toward the others and whistled, waving their arms in the air until the room settled.

John Russe, owner of the Provincetown dragger *John David* stepped to the front of the room. "Welcome. We are here tonight to plan a celebration." Some clapping and a murmur of voices filled the room. Everyone fell silent as John continued, "Our community has shared in prosperity because of the fishing fleet, and at the same time we are feeling the sadness because our neighbors have lost so much in the September 21st hurricane."

There was a soft shuffling throughout the room. "Our town came through the storm far better than our fellow fishermen to the south. The men in this room are here tonight because we thought we could help those less fortunate. The money we raise with this dance will be given directly to organizations dealing with relief efforts such as the Red Cross and Saint Peter's Lady's Aid Society." He let this sink in and then continued his prepared speech. "We're going to need help with advertising, refreshments, music, and anything else you can think of. There are sign-up sheets at the table in front with the names of committees, or you can write in any suggestions you have. There's coffee and baked goods near the door." The men in the room began talking to one another, drowning out John Russe's speech. The fishermen were tired and getting restless.

The Fishermen's Association secretary, Joe Thomas stood up, whistling and waving his arms. "Hold on, he's almost finished. Let Captain Russe finish." Joe's voice carried over the crowd. The men in the room stopped talking, leaving a sudden stillness.

John Russe finished with, "I'd like to thank you all for coming and for helping. Each committee will set it's own meeting place and time. Chairpersons will meet later to pull it all together. If you want to sign up, that would be great. I'm done now."

Manny always kept an eye out for business opportunities. He could see that helping the fishermen by sending out mailings asking for donations would be good for the town, and in turn, good for him. A murmur of voices went through the overheated room. Men began moving around, talking in groups, passing one another, nodding, and stopping to shake hands. A few headed for the door.

Provincetown's population was at an all time high with four thousand year-round residents. Townspeople knew each other through marriage, church, school, and community organizations. A large portion of the inhabitants' livelihood came from the harvest of fish and seafood, directly and indirectly. Draggers, trap boats, and a growing number of boats used for lobster trapping and setting long lines of hooks, all called Provincetown home. Manny's Ship Chandlery was showing a profit this year. With more fish coming to the wharfs, more new businesses were opening. Many men belonged to the fishermen's association. Other vessels came to the big open harbor: coastal schooners, ferries with commerce and tourists, sailing vessels, and yachts of all sizes filled the harbor during warmer months.

Prosperity in the fishing industry connected the town businesses in a way that everyone understood, but no one could explain. C.L. Burch's groceries, Bill's Diesel Service, Crowley Ice Co, J. Hilliard Coal and Wood, B.H. Dyer Hardware & Cordage, The Cape End Motor Co, and businesses too numerous to count, were directly impacted by the amounts of fish brought to the wharfs. And Provincetown was growing.

Manny leaned against the wall watching Frank Rosa walk toward him followed by a man Manny didn't know. "Hi Manny." Frank said, "This is Carlos Suvera. He's one of Provincetown's newest arrivals. He just bought a Chevy truck from Duarte Motors, and he's hoping to haul fish and freight." More fish meant new jobs and more money to town. New houses were being built. New cars and trucks crowded the streets. Manny liked how the town felt alive and prosperous. The country was in an upswing, pushing out of the great depression.

Frank headed toward the front of the room. Manny turned to the stranger, "Are you trucking fish?" Manny took note of the clean-shaven square jaw, pressed shirt, and manicured fingernails.

The newcomer answered, "I now own two trucks and I'm looking to expand my business. I bring dry goods, rum, and cigarettes from Boston. I'd like to return to the city with fish." He held out a pack of Double Mint chewing gum and offered a slice to Manny, who shook his head. The new-comer continued, "There's lots of competition for the fish, and being new in town doesn't help." Carlos looked around the room then said, "This is a good thing you're doing here. I thought I'd help out and get to meet some of the fishermen. How about you, are you a fisherman?" He slipped his gum back into his pocket and a jingle of loose change could be heard.

"Yes this dance is a good thing, and no, I'm not a fisherman. I sell what they need." Manny looked around the room. Merchants understood the banter, talking about weather, families, and news of the day was part of a shopkeeper's life, but Manny was tired. He was not up for small talk this evening. He said, "If you'll excuse me, I think I'll head up to the front and sign up. It's nice to meet you. Good luck with your new business." The men shook hands and Manny headed to the front of the room to see the lists.

Manny noticed that Frank Rosa the barber, Jimmy Sousa the fish buyer, and Sivert Benson an insurance salesman, had signed under the heading ADVERTISING. Manny added his name. He knew Jimmy Sousa and Sivert Benson by sight only. Neither man came into his store. Frank Rosa cut his hair four times a year and they had spoken many times. It was unlikely that this group of men would come together in any other way and Manny was looking forward to getting to know them better.

When Manny stepped up to the table a conversation was already in progress. He heard Frank say, "The news from Europe has me concerned. I understand that Czechoslovakia is now a part of Germany, some sort of pact of non-invasion. And then there's Spain's civil war." Frank spoke to many men while cutting their hair. He listened to the radio and he heard differing opinions as he used his shears and combs. Frank spoke quietly, "My oldest son will graduate this year." He looked at Manny. "Same class as your daughter Mary."

The barber looked at the others, "He'll be eligible for the Army and is talking about enlisting. My wife and I are trying to talk him out of it." Frank frowned and said, "And I read in the paper that China is having problems with Japan." He frowned as he shook his head.

Each of the men had their own concerns about what was happening on the other side of the world. Many families in Provincetown had relatives living in Europe. Sivert Benson added, "The problems in Europe and Asia don't concern us. It's local problems we need to address. Let President Roosevelt keep an eye on things. Keep your kid home, Frank." Sivert loosened his necktie. "Put him to work. Jimmy Sousa could find them a job, isn't that right, Jimmy?"

"Strong men are always welcome in the fish business," Jimmy replied. "I watched Captain Cordiero unload a trap boat that was filled to the gunnels, just this morning. It took four strong men using ropes, a block, and tackle on a gin-pole to hoist the heavy boxes up onto Macara's Wharf, must have been five thousand pounds." The talk always came around to fish when town businessmen got together. "Send that boy to see me, I'll find work for him." Jimmy Sousa was known around the waterfront as Jimmy-the-fish-buyer. He took the cigar out of his mouth and continued, "You know there are seventy-five fishermen who work the weirs. And there are twenty-nine draggers with many crewmen, and three hundred more men and women are employed at the ice plants." Each of the men in the room that night had made a profit during the past year and most of it came from the boats that called Provincetown home. The others listened.

"We may be a small town on the end of a sand spit, but we deliver fish all over the east coast. If war comes, and I sure hope it doesn't." the fish buyer tapped the end of his cigar, "Fish prices will go up. We'll be supplying fish to the Army and the Navy."

When Jimmy began talking about the price of fish at ten cents a pound, Manny decided to leave. It had been a long day and he needed fresh air. Pulling up his collar against the biting north wind he walked the three blocks to his home. The building was nestled between water and street with the Segura family on one side and the lawyer's office of James A. Vitelli on the other. His property contained Manny's Ship Chandlery on the first floor, street-side. Their kitchen was at the back, on the waterside, with the family living arrangements on the two floors above. Stored in the basement that the family called the marine room, were the barrels of nails, tar, pitch, and oakum that untwisted cotton-rope used for packing into the seams of wooden ships. There were coils of hemp rope, glass floats, shackles, fids, iron rings, and hooks. The shop contained thousands of items used by fishermen and mariners. Mending twine, jig hooks, gloves, boots, oiled-cloth jackets, and sailcloth shared the space with tools like planers, adzes, chisels, and awls.

Manny entered the shop and paused to take in the pungent smell of tar, pine, and wood. There was a hint of fish, possibly brought in by a crewman who stopped to pick up an order or sometimes to drop off the catch of the day. It was a fleeting prescient scent as if carried from afar on salt air, a comforting smell. He locked the door behind him and then remembered the guest in his office, a minor inconvenience. It gave him a gnawing in his belly. He wished the man would leave.

Chapter 5

The next morning the bell on the front door sounded as Davy Souza came into the ship chandlery bringing the aroma of salt, fish and cigarettes with him. In the past month Davy came and went frequently, at whim, like a neighborhood cat. "The wind is keeping the fleet tied to the dock. Just as well because this morning my crewman and I had to rescue our dory from the beach near the Provincetown Inn." Davy said with a singsong style of voice. He had a smile on his lips. He took off his cap and stuffed it into the pocket of his jacket. "How's Mrs. Diogo? How are Mary and the girls?"

"They're fine." The shopkeeper knew many of the Provincetown captains and crews that came into the shop. Some stayed to talk, while others said little as they pointed out what they needed. Davy Souza was one of the youngest captains. He didn't talk much, but he asked all kinds of questions. Manny had a hunch about Davy's visits to the chandlery. He came in for more than a hook or another pair of gloves. He'd been coming into the chandlery almost daily for something. The shopkeeper wondered if Davy was going to ask permission to take Mary out. Manny didn't like the idea of his daughter dating. Removing the thoughts of Mary he said, "What happened to your dory?"

"It's a mystery. No lines chaffed, but we got her back. No harm, no foul." Davy and Jimmy had spent half a day rescuing the skiff. They rolled it up the beach to check for damage then put it back in the water, and rowed it to the wharf, tying it alongside the fishing boat.

Manny interrupted Davy's thoughts about his skiff, "It seems our guest doesn't speak much English. We were wondering if you could you help us out and translate? We'd like to ask him some questions about his family so we can get in touch with them."

The fisherman was anxious to help. "I'm a little rusty now that Papa is gone, but I think I can interpret." Manny nodded his head and the men went through the hall to the office. Davy sat on the chair next to the cot.

Manny leaned against his paper filled desk. He knew he'd have to get in to the office soon to keep up with the invoices and bills. As Manny watched the two men he was struck by the idea that the two fellows were about the same age. The conversation was rapid in a language that had familiar musical sounds. Manny recognized some of the phrases having heard these same words when he was a child. He was third generation Portuguese-American and he had been encouraged to speak only English. Davy nodded his head, understanding, and then asking questions in short sentences.

When the voices ceased, the fishing Captain turned and looked up. "His name is Alonzo Rodrigues, and he has recently come from the Azores. He said he has no family in Provincetown." Davy looked up at Manny, "He said he is a fisherman. He doesn't want to make any trouble and wishes to thank the family for taking him in. That's it in a nutshell." Davy Souza stood up. The patient closed his eyes, pulled the blanket over his shoulders, and rolled toward the wall.

Davy spoke in subdued tones, "He said he came to town to find work and got caught in the storm."

"We'll let him rest," the older man said, "thanks Davy." Manny patted the patient on his arm and the two men left the room.

Manny closed the door. They walked toward the shop. Davy said, "I don't think he gave us the whole story. I'd be glad to help again." He paused to think about the words that had been spoken during the interview. "I think he speaks more English than he lets on, but if he is as he says, he'll get a job when he's feeling better."

They shook hands in the chandlery. Davy Souza hesitated, then slowly brought his eyes up to look at Manny, "Mr. Diogo, I was wondering if I could ask your permission to take Mary out to the movies this weekend?"

Manny had been expecting this and thought he knew what he was going to say, but he found himself stumped for words, "Well Davy, I don't know what to say. I'm not sure how I feel about that. I'll have to speak to my wife and then I'll let you know." His second thought was about Mary. What would she say? "Have you spoken to Mary?" After the enthusiastic fishermen shook his head no, Manny continued, "We'll talk again."

Davy Souza was nervous. He was shy when he spoke about Mary and in a strange way he was relieved that he didn't have to face her, not just yet. Building up his confidence took time. "Well that's fine, thanks and if you need me to speak to the man in the office again, let me know." He was gone into the darkening afternoon after saying goodbye.

In the days that followed, using the Portuguese language, hand signs and a bit of English, Alonzo told the family about where he was from. He left his island home after his parents died. The family boat was sold to pay debts. His story was not much different from other immigrants who had settled the shores of North America. "No work," he told them. He made no mention of how he'd come to Provincetown. He said he was a fishermen and thought he could find work. Although his story was not complete it had a ring of truth. The Diogo family accepted his narrative and the responsibility of helping the man get well. Manny felt unsure about the arrangement, but said nothing. He was uncomfortable having this man, a complete stranger, living in the house. The shopkeeper decided that Alonzo should keep to himself while he stayed with them, and that the man's business was none of his. They would help get him on his feet and out the door.

No one in the family gave a thought about mentioning their houseguest to their friend James Crowley. There was no reason to doubt what the immigrant said. They understood the kind of hardship and loss that drove men to seek new lives. It didn't concern Manny how the man made his living or where he'd come from. Manny asked their guest to remain in the office so as not to interrupt the family's daily routine. For the first week he kept to himself, taking his meals in the small room off the hall. During the second week Alonzo was stronger, alert, and growing healthier by the day and Eleanor invited him to join the family at the supper table. Everyone responded to his ready smile.

Mary kept glancing at the man. He was dressed in clothes supplied by her father, no doubt from the shelves in his store. She peeked at him whenever she thought no one was watching, but she did not speak directly to him. Hardly a word passed between them. Her younger sibling, Emily, on the other hand, was as curious as a cat and continually asked questions like, "Will you come back to visit us? What did your mother die from? Can I go fishing with you? Are you a

Catholic? Do you have a girlfriend? Do you own a boat and what is the name of your boat?" Sometimes she would get an answer, but mostly Alonzo would speak to her in Portuguese. Then Emily would stomp her feet and run up the stairs. The youngest, Juliana liked to laugh with Alonzo or at him, but Alonzo didn't seem to mind. After two weeks of good food, a warm bed, and life with the Diogo family, they were saying goodbye to a healthy Alonzo, twenty-four, born on the Island of San Michael, and a fisherman by trade. They had mixed feelings about seeing him leave, each with their own thoughts.

Davy offered Alonzo a job on the *Fanny Parnel*, telling the now recovered fisherman that he was in need of crew because Whiting was showing up on the Middle Bank. Alonzo moved into a room-by-the-week in the center of town, close to the railroad wharf. He was looking healthy, happy, and handsome when the family said goodbye. Manny noted the simple, tenuous smiles and handshakes that his daughters offered the young man as he left and he took note of the way his oldest daughter looked at their guest. It unsettled him. Eleanor put together a sea bag for the boy: a woolen sweater and pants, socks and long johns. She placed a pair of boots on top and told her husband it was their Christian duty. She took his now dry wool jacket from the hall closet and watched his eyes light up when he took it from her. It was the jacket that he had on when he arrived at their door. "*Obligado,*" he said.

Manny was the only one who was happy to see him go. He left on Monday, October 30, disappearing into the town. Eleanor went back to her household chores and painting in the attic when she could find the time. Manny worked in the chandlery and began cleaning up his office. The household routines returned. The girls sang along with the tunes they heard on the radio. When Duke Ellington and his orchestra played *It Don't Mean a Thing if It Ain't Got That Swing* - the house would thump and bump from the three girls jumping around the living room. The girls sang along with the songs from Tommy Dorsey orchestra *Our love* and *Music Maestro Please*. A favorite of the girls' was *Puttin on the Ritz* with Harry Richman. The family gathered in the living room each evening to listen to the world news and stories from "Amos n' Andy."

The holidays were coming, Thanksgiving, then Christmas, and finally in January they would dance the night away at the Fishermen's Ball. No one spoke to Mary about going to the dance. It would wait, and be given to her as a gift, a surprise during the Thanksgiving holiday. Mary asked her parents about the big dance, telling about friends who were going, but her parents just smiled and said they would have to wait to see what the rules would be. Her father thought Davy Souza might ask to take her, but so far he hadn't said a word.

"She is almost the same age as I was when I married you." Eleanor said to Manny. "She's blossoming, a woman with dreams." What they didn't know was that Mary had looked into the eyes of a stranger and found him mysterious, fascinating and seductive. She was tempted by the forbidden, exotic thoughts of sex. Her parents did not know that their daughter looked for him, slowing her steps as she neared the wharf, watching the boats coming and going. A few days after he had left their home, Mary's vigilance paid off. She was a block from her home and recognized him walking on the opposite side of the street. She called to him, "Hello Alonzo."

His eyes came up from the sidewalk, "Mary, hello. Is good to see you. I am fishing." His English was improving. His smile was wide. "I bring fish to family." Mary watched him cross the empty roadway to walk beside her. When they reached the chandlery he followed her down the ally to the beach and up the back stairs to the kitchen where Eleanor and Manny sat at the kitchen table. Alanzo lifted the string of codfish, presenting it.

Manny rose and shook his hand, thanking him. I'll put the fish in the sink. How've you been?"

Alonzo told them that his job was good and that he was grateful to them for their help. In his broken

English he said he would like to return the cost of the clothing as soon as he was paid. Manny began to protest, but changed his mind and said nothing. When Alonzo got up to leave Mary got up to follow him out. Her father stood at the same time and said, "I'll walk Alonzo out through the shop and close up after him. Mary, help your ma."

Manny suspected that something could develop between his daughter and Alonzo. "Thank you for the fish. Goodbye, Alonzo." He hoped he'd seen the last of him.

The immigrant nodded his head and was gone. When the door closed Alonzo turned toward the town's center. He passed shops, restaurants, and townsfolk on their way home, or out for an evening meal. As he approached the corner of Standish and Commercial streets, a stranger stepped from the side of the First National Food Store. He had the olive complexion and dark eyes of Portuguese or Italian ancestry. His build was short and muscular, like that of the local fishermen, except he was clean-shaven, well dressed and smelled of money. They walked together a few paces, moving in the same direction. Alonzo became nervous.

They looked briefly at each other. "Watch where you're going," the man said as he moved ahead and crossed the street. A shiver of suspicion ran through Alonzo. He was uneasy, but he didn't recognize the face. Alonzo noticed the quality clothing, a black wool cashmere topcoat, a fine felt hat. The scent of a good cigar hung in the air after he'd passed. Alonzo pulled up the thick collar of his jacket. Strangers made him nervous. He looked over his shoulder, glad that the man was gone.

He would buy a beer before hitting his bunk. He was feeling good about his choice to stay and begin fresh in Provincetown. Things were picking up for the immigrant. He liked that many of the town's fishermen spoke Portuguese. His new friends had helped him, he was earning a good wage and he knew the Diogo girl was flirting with him. This was a good place to start over. He would not let fear ruin his daydreams. He put the stranger out of his mind and headed to the pool hall.

Manny and Eleanor heard nothing more about Alonzo for several weeks. Thanksgiving arrived at the Diogo home and was made special when Mary was told that she would attend the Fishermen's Ball with her parents. The younger girls were disappointed but basked in the glow that radiated from Mary. The family broke into cheers, laughter, and hugs. It would be a short-lived happiness.

Chapter 6

Manny continued attending the weekly meetings where men sat around tables in an open room, discussing their part in making the fundraising and dance a success. One evening the advertising committee spoke about the brochure that they were developing. They began by drawing up a list of all the businesses in town, adding to it continuously for the past hour. They sent letters explaining the Fishermen's Ball, the booklet and tickets. The proceeds would go to relief efforts in New Bedford, the Cape and Island, and especially the families of fishermen who had lost their boats in the hurricane.

Talk about the dance came to an end when Sivert Benson said, "I read in the Standard Times that The Army Corp of Engineers is going to build jetties on the east end of town, near the Cold Storage building. Rocks from Maine are sent by barge and will be used for protecting the shorefront properties and the harbor. The federal government will be paying for most of it. I think it's a good idea."

Jimmy interrupted, "Not to change the subject, but I hear that Selectman Lewis got up at their meeting and said he feels that Railroad Wharf is the property of the people of Provincetown and it shouldn't be exclusively leased to anyone." He stopped to see if the others knew that the SS Steel Pier Company was asking to lease the whole of Railroad Wharf. The men nodded their approval. Jimmy continued, "Glad to hear the selectman said no to private ownership."

Manny noticed the room was beginning to empty. "Well if there's nothing more, I think I'll be heading home," he said. Manny left at the same time as Frank Rosa. They walked one behind the other down the outside stairs.

At the foot of the steps they paused and Frank put his hand on Manny's arm. He said, "Manny, I see that fellow you took in is recuperating nicely, he looks healthy. I saw him walking with your oldest daughter last Saturday afternoon. They looked like good friends, arm in arm. I understand he's a good fisherman."

Manny's eyes widened, "Yes, I guess he's doing well." He pulled his hat down. "I'll see you next week." Taking long strides, he headed east. Manny had strong feelings about his daughters and how they should be spending their time. There was no justification, and yet he didn't want the man around Mary. Something had to be done to nip this in the bud.

Later, when the house was quiet, Manny spoke to his wife. He told her what Frank had said. There was concern in his voice, "You've got to tell Mary she can't continue to see Alonzo. She would be throwing her life away if she takes up with him. He's too old for her. She's too young. I don't want Mary seeing him."

Sitting up on the side of the bed his voice grew louder, "She's got schooling in Hyannis next fall. Tell her, oh I don't know. Just tell her it's not a good idea. He's transient and will most likely be moving on."

Eleanor was surprised by his words. "Perhaps you're jumping to conclusions. After all, he was a guest here and she has every right to talk to the man. One walk on a Saturday does not make it anything else. You are naturally concerned for her and I understand that." Eleanor spoke slowly, "Mary may be a bit romantic, but we've got to trust her. She has a good head on her shoulders." Eleanor always looked to the bright side. She said, "Stop worrying. I'll talk to her." Eleanor slipped under the covers.

On the evening of December 5, 1938 the family had finished their supper and retired to the upstairs rooms. Manny was collecting an extra bundle of wood from the stack in the kitchen when he heard a pounding on the shop door. The banging caused the bell inside the shop above the door to vibrate, giving a small jingle. There stood Alonzo in rubber boots and heavy wool jacket. He had his hat in his hands, "Please, I need to speak to Mary."

Manny was too surprised to answer. He stepped aside and the fellow walked across the threshold. Manny closed the door and turned to see his daughter.

71

She looked more woman and less girl and Manny knew in his heart that it might be too late to keep them apart. He would leave them alone for five minutes. The shopkeeper sighed, knowing he would have to speak to his daughter about her future and the sooner the better. He would speak to Alonzo next.

"Five minutes," Manny said and turned away with a scowl on his face.

The two young people spoke in whispered voices. Within minutes Alonzo was gone and Mary was running up the stairs, crying. In bursts, between tears and sobs she told her mother that Alonzo had come to say goodbye. "He said he had to leave. I don't understand." Eleanor did her best to calm her daughter. She handed her daughter one of her father's white handkerchiefs, she held her daughter in her arms before laying her down and covering her with a quilt. When Mary had fallen into a deep sleep her mother left the room.

Eleanor was shaking her head when she said to her husband, "He seemed like a good boy, Manny. I saw him in church last Sunday. Why is he suddenly leaving?" Eleanor's eyebrows came together. "He was always so nice and polite when he was here."

"Maybe he didn't have papers." Manny was thinking of the stranger's story and was again doubtful that he spoke the truth about everything. "Maybe he was afraid someone would turn him in because he is here illegally." Manny's face was serious. "The immigrant wanted to move on. Let's leave it at that. Frankly, I'm glad to see him go." He thought for a moment about Mary and then whispered to his wife, "If that fellow has laid a hand on my daughter, I'll throw him off the wharf on a cold January night."

"Eleanor, please talk to Mary in the morning. Make sure she is ok. Do you know what I mean?" He paused, "I mean talk to her about sex."

Fred Salvador came to the chandlery after lunch the following day to place an order. A few minutes later Manny was surprised to see a police officer at the door. Sergeant Santos entered the store and asked if they could speak in the office, in private.

Manny turned to the fisherman, "I'll be right back."

"This way," he said to the Sergeant. Papers, books and stock items were in neat piles on the cot and filing cabinet, but the desk was clean. Neither man sat. The policeman closed the door.

Manny was not prepared for what Sergeant Santos said. "We've found a man, down on the beach under Sklaroff wharf and Chief Crowley wants to talk to you. He said to tell you to come by this afternoon."

"I don't understand. What has a man under the wharf got to do with me? The indigents who hang out under the piers are none of my business." Manny wanted to get back to the order that was waiting in the shop.

"I'm sorry, Mr. Diogo. Chief Crawley wants to talk to you about the fellow that stayed with your family a couple of months ago." The Sergeant looked at the floor, doing his best to be kind and official at the same time.

Manny stood very still. His first thought was that Alonzo would continue to create problems, even after he had left their home, and then he thought of his daughter. A feeling he'd had before came back to him. Alonzo was trouble. Manny wanted a few answers before he would agree to close the shop. He didn't like the thought that he might have to bail Alonzo out of jail. Why hadn't James just called him? Why the visit from Sergeant Santos?

Manny asked, "Are you saying Alonzo is in trouble?" Manny did not like the idea of getting involved with helping the man again. Manny raised his voice. "Can you at least tell me what's going on?" He was annoyed at the interruption.

The officer straightened his shoulders and said, "Mr. Diogo, a man is dead."

As if the policeman had used a foreign language, the two said nothing and just looked at each other. Manny knew that people came and went along the piers. Boats appeared during storms for refuge, sometimes to unload a catch of fish, or to buy supplies, and then disappear across the water. There had been accidents in the past, a misstep off the wharf.

"How is Alonzo involved in this?" The shopkeeper waited.

"You'll have to speak to Chief Crowley." The policeman raised his hands palms out. He was all business.

Manny took a breath, "Are you saying Alonzo is involved?" He couldn't believe the words coming from his mouth.

The policeman stood perfectly still. And then in a firm voice he said, "The chief said to tell you he wants to talk to you."

Manny opened his office door, "Okay Sergeant, tell him I'll be at his office after I take care of a few things here."

Passing coils of rope, boxes of shackles, and Freddy Salvador, captain of the *Stella*, the policeman left the chandlery. The door gave a jingle. Unaware of the tension growing in Manny's chest, Captain Salvador had been walking around the store with a paper in his hand. The calloused fingers and thumb seemed too swollen to hold such a delicate slip. Freddy's large bicep muscles bulged against his woolen shirt as if he were growing out of his clothing. The captain was affectionately called "Henry the Eighth" around the wharf. The fisherman was surprised to see a policeman come into the shop. "If there is anything I can help you with, don't hesitate to ask," Fred looked around the shop, then handed his list to Manny. Freddy is a high-liner, respected captain and fishing boat owner who Manny knew to take life as it came. He caught his share of fish and was always there to lend a hand whether on the wharf, in church, or to help a neighbor. The hardworking captain was also a member of the Fishermen's Association and a committee member for the Fishermen's Ball.

"Thanks Freddy. I think there's been some misunderstanding," the shop owner said. Manny knew that everyone in town would soon know about the death so he told Fred Salvador about what the Sergeant had said.

"What a shame. It can't be good for anyone. I hope it isn't Alonzo. I hear he's a good deckhand." Captain Salvador knew most of the boat captains and crews. "He started out fishing with Davy Souza, but switched to a bigger boat, Joe Macara's Annabelle *R*." This was news to the shopkeeper. The fisherman continued, "I've seen the boy around Railroad Wharf. He's been fishing steady for the past couple of months. Besides if he'd had an accident we'd have heard about it by now." Captain Salvador lowered his voice. "It was probably somebody else, from a transient boat, a freak accident." His head bounced a few times on his thick neck.

Manny took the list and shook Freddy's hand. "Can you come back later? I'll have this put together for you by tomorrow."

"There's no hurry. I'll send one of my crew to pick it up in the morning." The Captain tipped his Portuguese fishermen's hat.

The idea that the person who died might be Alonzo began to take shape in the shopkeepers mind. Manny felt a bit confused. He said, "Thanks for the offer of help and let's hope we don't need any. It must be a mistake." The fishermen nodded again and left the store.

The thought that he was connected in some way to the dead man was unnerving. He put the closed sign in the window and locked the front door, and then went to find his wife. He didn't like interrupting her when she was in her attic room. His voice echoed in the hallway. "Eleanor," He called as he climbed the steps, wishing he didn't have to say anything. The furrowed brow and scowl across his face was enough for his wife of eighteen years to see that something was wrong.

She wiped her hands on her apron and said, "Come up. What's going on?" Her questions were answered as Manny slumped into the soft overstuffed chair that he had managed to carry into the attic last spring. He stared at the floor for a moment, and then raised his eyes to meet hers.

"Sergeant Santos just left the shop. Seems the body of a man has been found under a pier on the west end. The Sergeant didn't say who it is, but the chief wants to speak to me." He sighed, "Alonzo may be involved, or worse, he may be dead."

There was a sharp intake of breath and Eleanor turned pale. "Oh! Let's hope not," she said.

"Santos wouldn't give me any details. I have to see James, I'm going now." He reached out for her and they sat together without speaking. Then Manny continued, "We'll talk when I get back. I've got a committee meeting at the Legion Hall at four." He paused and took a deep breath, letting it out slowly. "I was going to close the store a little early today anyway." He kissed his wife and left her staring after him. There was nothing more to say.

Chapter 7

James Crowley had been the town's Police Chief for seven years. He loved his job. Crowley was born in Provincetown. After high school he did a hitch in the Army for Uncle Sam, and then went to the state police academy, before returning to his hometown. He was well liked by the town's citizens, most of them. Crowley took his allegiance to protect and serve his community seriously. The crimes that took place in this coastal village usually involved domestic violence, alcohol, theft, and the occasional fight between fishermen.

Earlier that morning the chief had been called from his warm bed to the pier that held the cold storage building of Cape Cod Fisheries. A local dory-man who had been heading for his fishing boat in the pre-dawn hours called to summon help. The chief walked two blocks and then passed through an alley leading to the water. Frank Cordiero was waiting when he arrived. Crowley saw the fisherman wave his arm in the twilight sky. He was standing at the head of an old wooden pier that jutted away from the land into the water like a dead-end road, going nowhere. A large fish house, appearing to lean toward the east due to the angles in the roof, cast a shadow across the water in front of him. The chief strained to see where the fisherman pointed. Captain Cordiero greeted the police chief and spoke softly as they walked toward the water. "When I realized it was a body next to the pilings, I knew I had to get you." Daylight was seeping into the sky as the two men joined three others who were standing in a semi-circle facing the water. The chief knew immediately that the man on the beach was beyond medical help.

"Can anyone tell me what happened? Do any of you know who this is?" He recognized the men around him, making a mental note of each, Big Billy Segura, Tony Thomas, and Manuel Viegas. They shook their heads almost in unison, saying only, "No." Puffs of white mists from their mouths evaporated into the cold air.

Chief Crowley's mind was racing. He bent close to the man. His clothing was waterlogged. His wool shirt squished when he touched it. There was no blood to be seen. The skin on his face was gray, his eyes glassy. His shirt was ripped. Crowley pushed a piece of his shirt aside. There seemed to be some kind of wound in the man's mid left chest, a cut that no longer bled. He told himself not to jump to conclusions. He'd have Doc examine the body. The chief turned away from the dead man and walked back to the group of men. He spoke to Frank Cordiero, "Tell me how you found him."

The fisherman had his hands balled in fists, hanging against his solid body. He was wearing the peaked hat that the Portuguese fisherman preferred and had the collar of his slicker pulled up to his cheeks. Frank explained that his boat was hanging on a trip-line off the pier. "I came for the dory. We're not going out today. The traps are out of the water and I wanted to bring the dory up onto the beach before winter sets in. Big Billy was going to give me a hand pulling it up at high tide." The man was used to taking his time, telling stories around the potbellied stove in the shed on the wharf. He paused, looked at the police chief, then out toward the water. "The sun was just below the horizon. I was pulling in the line to bring the dory to the wharf when I looked down toward the bulkhead." Captain Cordiero pointed to where a trip-line was tied to the wharf attached to his small boat and then in the opposite direction. He took a deep breath. "For some reason, I looked up toward the street. That's when I saw him."

The fisherman folded his arms across his barrel shaped chest. His head shook from side to side as he gathered his words. "I didn't see him when I came for the boat. I walked up the pier from street-side. Right over him, I guess." He paused, "I re-tied the line and let the boat go back because something didn't look right. I wasn't sure what I was seeing, thought maybe a dead seal or a Minke whale. Too cold for anyone to be sleeping out there on the beach, and it wasn't moving." Frank shuddered. "I got to him as quick as I could," the fisherman's voice was raspy, "But it looks like he's been with the angels for awhile."

The other fishermen told the chief that they hadn't seen anything and they didn't know the man. They had arrived a few minutes before, also heading to the boats. Big Billy Segura confirmed that he was there to help pull the dory up above the tide line. "We're taking the boat out of the water, for the cold season," he said. "We've all had a look at the corpse. No one knows him."

The two other men shook their heads, made the sign of the cross, and stood at the edge of the scene. Manuel Viegas owned the *Etelvina V.* and Tony Thomas was with Captain Viegas. They were planning to row out to the boat, check the lines and make sure there was no water in the bilge.

Captain Cordiero mentioned to the chief that the Diogo family had helped out a stranger, new in town, just a couple of months ago. "Could be him, but I didn't know the fellow. Davy Souza has a new fisherman working with him as well, but I couldn't tell you if this was him." The fisherman pushed at the sand with his boot and said, "They tie their boat on Fishermen's Wharf, so I don't get to see them often."

The chief took a small notepad from his pocket. "Can you stay here for a few more minutes, while I look around?" Frank and the other men stood perfectly still, as if rooted in the sand. Their heads bowed out of respect. They kept their thoughts to themselves and their hands in their pockets. To keep warm the men occasionally moved their feet.

Chief Crowley ducked as he stepped into the shadowed area under the wharf. It took a moment for his eyes to adjust to the darkness. Scattered on the sand were a few rusty hoops, remains of discarded barrels. An overturned bucket with a hole in the bottom, and a short piece of hemp line lay on the sand. Nothing else was visible. The policeman looked at the tarred poles that held up the pier. They rose to planks twelve feet above his head. The tide would cover this place in a few hours. He removed his hat and looked up at the underside of the massive structure. It was too dark to see. He'd take a closer look when the sun was higher, both on top of the wharf and under it.

The chief's thoughts were that the man had fallen from the wharf into the water. He must have struck something in the fall. He could easily have drowned if the tide were high. The water was too cold to survive more than a few minutes, especially if no one saw or heard him go in. There are a few ladders on the wharfs, if he'd known where to look. The chief could see that the closest ladder was near the end of the pier, in deeper water. Crowley judged the body to be only ten feet below the high tide line. Maybe he tried to cling to a pole, but how long could a man last in this frigid water, especially if he'd struck a nail or spike on his fall from the wharf. Crowley muttered, "Any number of things could have happened." The chief stopped talking to himself, made a note on the pad to take a good look at the wharf when the sun was higher.

The chief slowly scanned the area. There were a number of lines going from the wharf to dories in deeper water, but nothing close to shore. The old pier was showing its age, tar squeezing from the timbers that grew sea life on the pilings. He searched around the body, then rolled the man over, and spent a minute digging at the sand under the body. There was nothing, just sand. When he stood up he realized that any footprints would have been washed away by the tide. The men surrounding the body had taken care of any that might have been missed by the water. The chief's breath was coming from his mouth in clouds of white vapor as he asked, "What time was the high tide last night?" There was a possibility that the body washed up, having fallen off a boat, and been brought onto land like so much flotsam.

The fishermen told him the tide was high at midnight and low at around 6 AM. "Almost dead low now," the fisherman said. "A fall off the wharf into the cold water with no one around, well, unfortunately, it wouldn't be the first time a fishermen's met his death through such an accident." Captain Cordiero made the sign of the cross.

The chief didn't share his knowledge about the cut on the dead man's chest. Whether the man fell from the wharf or from a boat it didn't matter. He didn't like it either way. No one had been reported missing to the Provincetown Police. He thought the body looked like it had been in the water for a while, water logged. Crowley made a note to ask the Doc. He wrote down everyone's names, the time, what he saw and didn't see. He looked again at the dead man, taking in the dark hair hanging over his eyes, the wool pants, and shirt. Crowley was thinking it was pretty cold to be out here without a jacket. And where were his shoes? He had on black wool socks, but no shoes, no boots. The body was curled in a fetal position around a piling, soaked and grey and as dead as the wood he seemed to be embracing. Chief Crowley said out loud, "Poor kid."

After a second look at the body Crowley asked Big Billy to go to the police station and tell the desk sergeant to get Mr. Richland. "Tell him to bring his hearse and tell him to call Doc Rice to meet us at the funeral parlor."

Mr. Richland arrived and the body was taken away. The chief told the fishermen to come to his office later that day. "I'd like you all to write up what you saw, even if you think its nothing." They nodded and went out to the dories leaving the chief to think about what had been said and what he'd observed. He scrutinized the area one last time before heading to Richland's Funeral Parlor out at the edge of town.

The chiefs suspicions were confirmed when he had a closer look at the body. A wound in the upper left chest, another gash in the abdomen, both appeared deep. The slash in the abdomen had ragged edges and it was open as if fish had already nibbled the edges. Crowley shuddered.

"Looks like either one of those cuts would be enough to kill him, never mind the cold water," Mr. Richland said. Before the undertaker pulled the cover over the body he added, "The wound in his chest looks enough to kill."

Chief Crowley didn't like what he was seeing or hearing. "Just the same, let's wait for Dr. Rice. You're jumping to conclusions. I'll have the doc do a thorough exam." The undertaker nodded, his head bouncing on his long thin neck as he left the room. The chief waited, wondering about the dead man. The doctor entered half an hour later, huffing and puffing, pulling off his overcoat. He said, "Sorry it took so long. I had to walk all the way. My son took the car to Boston. He was supposed to be back yesterday. He's gone and signed up for the Army, but never mind that now. I hear you've found a body." He'd been practicing medicine in Provincetown for thirty years and he thought he'd seen it all. As the sheet was lifted the doctor sucked in air, sharply. His face registered surprise like he'd been slapped. "I know this boy." He explained to the chief how he'd come to meet him and how he'd asked Eleanor and Manny to care for him.

When the doctor finished, the chief said, "I know you'll do a thorough exam. I'll need you to write up what you just told me about finding him at the chandlery last October. And please call the office when you're done here. I'll have someone come get you and drive you back to your office." The chief hesitated, let out a large breath and added, "I want to know exactly what killed him. I'd appreciate your opinion on this. And I don't need to tell you, the less said about this man, the better." Doc Rice nodded in the affirmative and Chief Crowley hurried from the chilly room.

Chapter 8

The walk to the Police Station took Manny Diogo ten minutes. He passed the homes of his neighbors, the Methodist Church, the Mayflower Gift Shop now closed until spring, the Portuguese Bakery with it's sweet smells melting into the street, and then past John A. Francis who waved at him from the large window advertising real estate and insurance. The street was empty, but the town was open for business.

The police department was located in a small basement area of the town hall with its entrance on Ryder Street at the side of the building. It was tucked underneath the stately structure that was built in 1886 after the old town hall on the hill burned to the ground. Town offices, a courtroom, and a grand auditorium occupied the space on the floors above the police headquarters. The shopkeeper went down four steps and opened the door. A pear shaped man wearing a uniform of dark navy blue with brass buttons down the front greeted him. "Chief's been expecting you, Mr. Diogo, go straight back." Ducking his head away from the water pipes that heated the building, Manny passed two empty holding cells. At the end of the cement hallway the door was open.

Chief Crowley was back at his desk, having skipped lunch. He was looking at what he'd written about the events of the morning, adding words as they came to him. He looked up. "Thanks for coming in Manny." The chief stood and they shook hands across the desk.

"I'm not going to beat around the bush. We've been friends most of our lives and I don't have any reason to think you had anything to do with what I'm about to tell you. Doc Rice said the body belongs to the fellow that was nursed back to health by your family last October." He watched Manny closely as he let this sink in.

Manny opened his mouth to speak, but nothing came out. He sank into the chair facing the desk.

"I'm sorry about this, Manny. I'd like to ask you a few questions and I was hoping you could give me a positive identification." Their eyes met. "I could use some background information about this man. No one seems to know much about him."

Manny shook his head like a horse chasing a fly away. He turned his face away from the chief, "God, this is awful. This is going to come as a shock to Eleanor and the girls. He doesn't have any family here, none that I know of. Alonzo comes from San Miguel." Manny looked up, "Are you sure it's Alonzo?"

Crowley nodded. "Doc Rice remembers him at your house at the end of October."

"What happened to him? Did he have an accident?" Manny paused trying to collect his thoughts, and then added, "I guess I don't really know too much about him. Eleanor may know his birth date and where he is from. I think he's twenty four." He stopped and slowly added. "My girls all seemed to have liked him."

Manny paused, cleared his throat then continued, "He brought fish to the house a few times. God this is awful. Oh, I forgot he stopped by a few nights ago, wanted to talk to..." He took a breath, "To bring us fish." Manny abruptly stopped speaking. His brow was furrowed and a look of confusion passed over his eyes. He spoke softly, "What happened? I understand that he's been fishing with Davy Souza on the *Fanny Parnell*. You should talk to Davy. Alonzo speaks mostly Portuguese, I mean spoke." He stopped again and then added, "Maybe you should speak to some of the Portuguese fishermen." This all ran from the shopkeeper's mouth in one breath as if he couldn't keep up with the words.

Manny decided not to bring up his daughter, the way she looked at the Alonzo when he came to the house, or the way she had reacted. He added, "He told us he was leaving town." Manny hung his head as if in prayer. His friend said nothing for a few moments.

Crowley stood up and came around the desk to stand next to his friend. "I'll see Davy Souza later when the boat gets back to the dock, he's out fishing. In the mean time would you mind coming with me over to Richland's? You're about as close as any family he had in town. I need someone to identify him, officially. We can talk on the way."

"Yes of course." Manny said. He'd seen dead people laid out for inspection, mostly his family and friends. Just this year he had attended the funerals of two good fishermen who had lived their lives the way they had wanted, both dying in old age. This was different, unsettling, and unnatural.

The old farmhouse on the Race Road had been converted into a funeral parlor. The basement was now the mortuary. The paved road ended just past the front door. The town was expanding. It wouldn't be long before the road would go all the way out to Clapper's Pond. There had been talk of it at the last Town Meeting.

The Chief opened the door without knocking and they walked in. Manny was not prepared for the stark room with cold cement floor, white walls and the smell of formaldehyde. A stick-like figure of a man with thick white hair combed high and away from his freshly-shaven pale face met them. Everyone knew Mr. Richland. There were nods.

"Chief" the undertaker said as he led them to a table, lifting the snow-white sheet.

Manny sighed. Alonzo looked smaller. His skin was grey, waxy, and bloated. He looked like he'd gained weight overnight, but there was no doubt. Tears sprung to his eyes like the rush of salt water on a high spring tide, surprising everyone in the room. "It's Alonzo Rodrigues. God rest his soul." The shopkeeper made the sign of the cross and then mumbled, "Can we go now? I need some air." The shopkeeper turned away from the body. "I've a meeting at the Legion Hall." Walking toward the door Manny said, "I feel like I'm dreaming." He jumped when the chief put his hand on his shoulder.

"I'm sorry about this. Is this the man that stayed with you?" Manny nodded yes. Crowley wished he didn't have to interfere in his friend's grief, but he needed to know certain things. "I need to talk to you again, Manny, tomorrow, my office, ten o'clock." It did not sound like an order, but it was, "I'll drop you off at the Legion Hall, or would you prefer to go home?"

Manny said, "I need to think about this. How will I tell the girls? I have a meeting about the ball. It's just across the street from your office."

Mr. Richland seemed unaware of the body next to them, "How's the planning for big dance coming along? My wife is looking forward to it already and it's still a month away."

Manny said something about January 19 and left the basement. He was thinking of the stranger who had washed up on his doorstep. The person they had come to know, even if superficially, who they had sheltered in their home, who now lay on a cold table at

Richland's. Manny pictured the stranger who he had carried up the stairs. He had a vision of him laughing at the table with his girls. There was a flash of thought that the man had brought turmoil and grief along with the laughter.

On the way back to town the two men talked. Manny asked, "How did he die?"

James told his friend that Alonzo had been found under the pier, but did not say more about the young man's death. "I'll be calling the State Police Office. This is an unexplained death." Manny looked up, as if to ask why, but kept silent.

The Chief asked if Manny had an address in Portugal? How long had he stayed with them? Did he know of anyone he was friendly with and where was he staying? With each question Manny shook his head. "One of the fishermen told me that Alonzo had been fishing with Davy Souza," the chief said, "But that he left Davy and went to work on the *Annabella R.* Do you know anything about that?"

"I knew Davy gave him a job. But the rest I don't know."

In a quiet voice the chief asked, "Do you think Eleanor or your daughter Mary can give us some information about Alonzo?"

Manny bristled, became defensive. He said, "No. I don't think so. Maybe Eleanor can help with some details." He had answered all the chief's questions as best he could. "I have to admit I really don't know much about the fellow. He spoke mostly Portuguese and I didn't pay much attention. He spent two weeks with us, two months ago, but it seems like two years now. I realize I don't remember much about him."

As they parted James said, "Talk to Eleanor and your daughters, maybe they can remember family, friends or anything else that could help." The chief let Manny out of the car at The Town Hall, thanking him. He leaned against the squad car and watched Manny cross the street and then Crowley headed to his basement office.

Manny turned away from the police station, his friend, and the Legion Hall. He walked in a daze toward the east end, for home. The sight of Alonzo's dead body had shaken him to his core. Assuming he'd had an accident, he turned his thoughts to his family. The way Mary had looked at the young man when he came to their house just a few nights ago. He had not told James about the visit, protecting his daughter seemed the right thing to do, unaware of the realities of the death.

Manny was a realist, seeing the good as well as the bad. His years dealing with captains, crewmen, and lumpers had given him insight into small-town life. Sometimes heavy drinkers would come into his shop asking for credit to buy a spool of twine and they would holler about lazy crews and no fish. There were the occasional fights that broke out on the wharf, anger and whiskey boiling over. He could understand how a fisherman could get drunk and fall off the wharf into the freezing water. The men in the fleet had rough times, weeks without pay, boats lost at sea, men who never returned. He walked with gloomy thoughts. This tragedy would affect them all in ways they could not begin to imagine.

Eleanor read the sadness on his face, greeting him with a hug that lasted longer than usual. When they separated, he looked into her eyes and said, "I'm sorry, it's Alonzo. He's dead."

Tears spilled down her face, "I was so hoping that it wasn't true." Manny held her. She dried her eyes on her apron and whispered, "I'll make tea." They sat together at the kitchen table without speaking until Manny broke the silence.

"How do you want to handle this with the girls?" He would do what his wife decided. "I know the girls were fond of him. It's going to be a shock for everyone. You were kind to him, Eleanor, you can be proud of how you helped him." Eleanor put her arms over her husband's shoulders and placed her cheek next to his.

Her voice was soothing, smooth and soft. "We should speak with Mary first, alone. The young ones will be sad and have questions, but it won't affect them in the same way. You must have seen how she's been mooning around here lately. This is going to be very difficult for her; she was very fond of him."

His head felt heavy. He felt sick to his stomach. "I have to see the chief again. He wants to know everything we can remember about the boy." Manny hesitated, "How close was Mary to him? The chief mentioned her. He may want to speak to her about their relationship."

Eleanor was surprised. "Why is he asking about Mary?" Her eyebrows rose. "She liked him. We all did. I don't know about any romance between them if that's what you mean. And what difference does that make anyway. It's none of his business."

Eleanor took a deep breath, "Why is James asking these questions? Mary is a dreamer, you know that." She looked out the kitchen window. "I don't believe she knew him any better than we did. And she certainly couldn't have had anything to do with Alonzo's death." She reached out her hand and Manny took it.

That evening the girls came bouncing into the kitchen as usual to share their day, tease each other, and eat. There was no moon, no stars shining through the kitchen windows, no music coming from the radio, and no smiles on their parent's faces. The room was lit by one electric light over the table. Eleanor added two kerosene lamps and a candle in the window that softened the room's atmosphere. A fire was burning in the cooker. She wished everything could continue for as long as was possible without this sadness of death entering their home. The dishes were cleaned and placed on the shelf. A look passed between the parents. Manny spoke, "Mary, your mother and I need to talk to you. Emily and Juliana please go upstairs. Get ready for bed. Your mother and I will be up to help in a few minutes." It must have been his tone of voice; the girls didn't say a word. They turned and climbed the stairs.

Mary frowned, glared at her parents, expecting something entirely different from what was said. "Mary, please sit down. I'm afraid we have some bad news." Manny spoke softly. "There's been an accident." He paused as if he didn't wish to continue. "Alonzo is dead."

Mary rose from her seat, "No, there must be some mistake. That's impossible. What are you saying?" Her eyes were wide open. "He's out fishing. It must be a mistake."

Her father spoke again, "There is no mistake. He's in God's hands now."

He reached out to her, but she pulled away and ran to the stairs, crying out, "This can't be true."

That night after the shock had worn off, sadness moved into their home. When everyone had time to understand what had happened, Manny sat at the edge of Mary's bed. She was wringing a handkerchief in her hands. Her eyes filled, still overflowing, but the sounds of sorrow had subsided. Manny took a deep breath. "Listen to me sweetheart. We are trying to piece together what happened to him. Some things can't be explained, but maybe you can help us." Manny hoped his daughter would not become hysterical. She remained speechless with large tears rolling down her cheeks.

"He was a good person, Daddy." A short intake of air and then she continued, "We talked. He wants a fishing boat for himself. It can't be him." Mary stopped and hiccupped.

"I'm afraid it's true." Manny hesitated, "I think Chief Crowley will want to talk to you about him."

A sigh that sounded like a moan came from Mary and then she whispered, "What happened? Can you tell me?"

"I don't know any of the details, but Chief Crowley is looking into it." Father and daughter sat quietly for some minutes. Mary leaned into her dad, laying her head on his shoulder. Manny felt the same tenderness that he'd felt on the day she was born. He put his arm around his daughter, knowing he would wait to talk with her about Alonzo. She felt so small to him. "I'm sorry," he said.

When her father had left the room, Mary thought about Alonzo. She pictured his face, remembering his smile and his kisses. She turned toward the wall and curled herself into a ball, folding into herself for protection against a harsh world. After a few minutes she reached around the bed and put her hand under the mattress, bringing out a coin that was heavy, shining gold with the profile of a man imprinted upon it. It warmed in her hand.

Chapter 9

The next day Manny sat opposite James Crowley. The usually neat desk was messy. The telephone was buried under newspapers. Notebooks containing the chief's scrawl lay on top, and a folder containing statements from witnesses was open. The two men had worry written on their expressions. The chief had not told Manny everything. He felt he owed his friend an explanation. "I've called the state police to get some help with this. They're sending someone, should arrive tomorrow." The chief knew he could trust Manny. They grew up knowing each other. Crowley pulled at the mustache above his mouth and continued, "This has me worried. I'll know more after the state guys take a look at the body." That was as far as their friendship would take him. "I know you don't want to hear this, but I need to talk to your daughter, Mary."

Manny bit the edge of his upper lip. His eyebrows knit together and he sat straighter in the chair. He did not speak.

The chief added, "She may know something about what this boy has been doing." He hesitated and then said, "I was told Mary and Alonzo have been seen together on a number of occasions." He let that sink in, waiting to see how Manny would react. His friend said nothing. Crowley continued, "Listen Manny, the boy spent time with your family. It's only natural."

The shopkeeper cleared his throat, "She liked him. We all liked him." Manny was becoming uncomfortable. "Now tell me, what has any of this to do with us, with Mary?" The chief looked across the desk. The friends sat quietly in the overheated office. Then as if a door had opened letting in a crack of light, Manny became aware of what his friend was telling him. "Are you saying it wasn't an accident?"

Chief Crowley frowned, "I'm not saying yes and I'm not saying no. I can only tell you that it doesn't look good."

Manny's eyebrows shot up. "He only spent two weeks with us, but okay, maybe he spoke to Mary. She was very upset when we gave her the news."

The police chief waited. Manny continued, "Alonzo told us that he came to Provincetown looking for work. He was caught in a storm and found shelter in the alley next to our house. When we found him he was clearly ill, Doc Rice asked if we could look after him. It was hypothermia and he was weak. We took him in. That's all I know." Manny sighed deeply, not wanting to bring his family into this and yet knowing there was no turning back the clock. "Maybe Eleanor or Mary can give you some information about him. Come to the house after supper tonight, seven o'clock." The men shook hands. They held them for longer than usual, something they hadn't done in years, not since James had left for the Army.

That evening, around the Diogo kitchen table the police chief joined Eleanor, Manny, and their eldest daughter. Mary's head was bowed as if unable to look into anyone's eyes. Eleanor had pulled her chair close and was holding Mary's hand under the table. Manny sat on her right with a pained expression on his face. The Police Chief had on a white shirt, a dark V-neck sweater, and a dark jacket. His topcoat hung on the hook next to the kitchen door. He sat opposite Mary.

"Mary, you know me. I'm a friend of your parents and the police chief. I'd like to ask you a few questions about Alonzo. Can you help me?"

The room was quiet. Outside the surf could be heard slapping the shoreline. Chief Crowley spoke in hushed tones, "I know all this has come as a shock, but I'd like to get some background information about Alonzo."

She appeared younger than her seventeen years, fragile. She looked left and then right at her parents. Her lower lip quivered as she whispered, "His English was very good and he was working to make it better. We laughed about some of the words he used." Mary began to tell them what she knew about Alonzo. "He said he grew up in the Azores off the coast of Africa. Everyone was poor." She stopped to catch her breath. "His mother died when he was fifteen and his dad when he was twenty years old. To pay the debts he had to sell his father's boat. He said he was not a farmer and did not want to grow grapes." The words seemed to roll out of her like a snowball down a hill, picking up in size, matter, and speed. "He left his home for a better life and found work on boats."

Manny was surprised by how much she knew that he didn't. He listened to what she had to say and kept his thoughts to himself.

"I remember he talked about the long distances that they went to catch fish, from the Azorean Islands to ports along the Mediterranean coast. Then he found a job on a trawler, a small freighter that carried trade goods. He left from the southern coast of France, a city called Marseille." The others waited without interrupting. "Alonzo said the ship crossed the Atlantic, went to an island to pick up rum. Mary stopped speaking, tears filled her eyes. Her mother stood up, placed hand on her daughter's shoulder, wanting the interview stopped.

Instead, the policeman put up his hand, his index finger raised, to signal Eleanor not to say anything. He asked Mary in a quiet voice, "Can you tell me the name of the boat he worked on?" She shook her head. "Do you remember anything more?" He waited for her to speak, but she did not. "Does he have friends here? What about family, do you remember the names of family?" He waited but Mary didn't speak. The chief chose his words carefully, "I understand he came into the shop the other night to see you, what did he say?"

Manny picked up his daughter's hand and said, "It will be alright, Mary. You can answer the chief. Did he tell you why he was leaving, or where he was going?"

The seventeen year old looked at her father, her mother, and then at Chief Crowley. She shook her head and whispered, "No. I don't know where he went or why he left. He said he had to go away for a few days but that he would be back." Mary was pulling at a white handkerchief that Eleanor had placed in her hands, "He told me some things about growing up on an island. He didn't have any family here in Provincetown and I don't remember the names of people in the Azores." Tears began to form and roll down her cheeks. "He said he was saving for a future. He wanted to settle down. He called Provincetown his harbor of refuge." This time her tears turned to sobs. The interview was over.

Manny walked Chief Crowley down the hall and through the store. The policeman said, "The way he showed up on your doorstep, so to speak, makes me wonder if he was running from something or someone. We're pretty sure he entered the country without papers or permission. Immigration has no record of him." The chief reached for the door handle, "Showing up on the beach, soaking wet, I don't think he could have walked from Boston. Right now it doesn't make much sense, but I'll talk to some of the fishermen and see if we can get more information." What the chief didn't say was that he believed Mary knew more than she was saying. This was not the time to press her, but he would see her again when the shock wore off.

When Chief Crowley had gone and their daughters were tucked under the covers, husband and wife sat together on the sofa near the Franklin stove, their bodies touching, as if to keep each other from falling over. Manny sighed, "James told me he didn't think Alonzo had an accident, not in so many words, but that's what he meant." He paused, "I wish I could keep you and the girls out of this, but it seems we're the closest thing he had to family on this side of the Atlantic." His words seemed too loud for the quiet house. He whispered, "I think it might be a good idea to keep Mary home with you, just for a few days. No school, no friends, and no going downtown alone." Eleanor's eyes widened and her mouth fell open. Manny continued, "This doesn't involve us directly. It's nothing to worry about, really." He held his wife's hand, squeezing it to reassure her. "It's just that she looks so fragile."

Eleanor said she understood. "We'll get through this. Christmas is just three weeks away, it will take everyone's mind off this death and we can concentrate on the birth of Christ. Seems like that would be best for our girls, don't you think?" Eleanor wanted the happiness that the family knew before Alonzo's death. Life would go on, she thought, but not in the same way.

The days that followed were gloomy, fitting right into the mood of the Diogo home. The temperature dropped. Gray skies brought snow and wind driven sleet, keeping most of the town's citizens indoors. There was a small notice in the newspaper about Alonzo, without much detail. There was no memorial service, no wake or burial announcement. The only mention of his name was said during prayers at Saint Peter's Church. The two younger sisters went to school, rehearsals for the Christmas show, and church on Sunday. Mary remained at home for a week, reading, sleeping and sometimes helping her mother, but now she was weeping less and helping around the house more.

The town was busy. People came in and out of the many downtown stores, some decorated with glitter, trees and angels. The town had a lively feeling as if anticipating that something important was about to happen. It seemed that this year because of all the talk about the big dance with a live band, the holidays were enhanced and the spirit of community took on a fresh face. The Depression that had been hanging over the country like a dark cloud seemed to be lifting. People had money in their pockets and smiles on their faces. Provincetown's citizens lived in a modest, self-contained manner, and now the village was invigorated, cheered and upbeat. Women were speculating about the upcoming Fishermen's Ball, what the band would play, who would attend, and what everyone was wearing.

The men spoke of the money being raised and how important it was to support other fishing communities. In contrast to the gaiety, a somber Mary told her parents she no longer wanted to go to the ball. Eleanor said nothing. Manny thought it was time to end the drama, but kept his thoughts to himself. The dance was a month away, enough time to change their daughter's mind. They agreed that the happy sounds of an orchestra would help her to move forward. It was time to put this episode to rest like a bad dream. Eleanor would have a talk with her eldest daughter.

Chapter 10

The shopkeeper went to the Legion Hall as usual on Monday, enjoying the company and discussions. Someone had decorated the large open room with paper chains made by the school children and a string of colored lights hung in the front windows, but the sight did not cheer Manny. He spotted Davy Souza sitting with a group of fishermen. He nodded, but didn't stop to chat.

Manny sat down with Frank, Sivert, and Jimmy-the-fish-buyer at a rectangular table. They were opening envelopes containing donations and requests for tickets. "We've had a good response from the fish buyers," Frank said. "There are twenty-seven requests for advertising from the trucking companies: The Atlantic Coast Fisheries, Cape Cod Fisheries, The Fish Forwarding Co, Beyer Fish from New York, Kurtz & Sons, J.A Rich Company from Boston, Berman Fish Co from the Fulton Market, and Sam Cahoon from Woods Hole, to name just a few of the companies that have sent money." There was excitement in his voice. "This money can't come soon enough for the hurricane victims."

Everyone at the table seemed to be enjoying the evening. "We've had responses from other businesses as well: insurance companies, shops, and restaurants, as well as individuals. The donations and ticket sales are strong." Sivert Benson was writing down names and numbers on a pad of paper, keeping track of what had been sent.

It had been three months since the hurricane and the towns to the south, hardest hit, still had not recovered. Reports in the Cape Cod Standard Times and the Boston Newspapers wrote of massive destruction along the south facing coasts. The storm that brought sustained winds over 100 mph was being called the storm of the century. The wind and high water wreaked havoc all along the Connecticut, Rhode Island, and southern Massachusetts coasts before it moved inland. Provincetown was spared the brunt of it. The small fishing port at the tip of Cape Cod suffered no loss of life. It was difficult for most of citizens of Provincetown to compare the reports in the news about the destruction with the minor inconveniences they had to overcome. The people felt they had much to be thankful for.

Sivert Benson spoke up, "Have you heard about the telephone and radio operators at the Long Point Radio Station?" He waited for everyone's attention.

"They helped clear thousands of emergency calls during the hurricane, forging a link of transmissions between the stricken districts and Boston. Governor Charles F. Hurley has commended Provincetown's own telephone operator, Matilda Montgomery and the others at the radio station for their actions during the hurricane. They may get a medal."

Everyone in the Legion Hall that night was aware of what had taken place during the hurricane, but now the death of a fisherman had taken over as local gossip. Out of respect for Manny no one spoke openly about the immigrant that he had helped, or about the questions that were mounting concerning his death. Most of the men in the room didn't know the dead man. Although curious, they resisted the urge to gossip.

Instead conversations about what had happened in other communities took everyone's attention. On the opposite end of the room Freddy Salvador was talking, loud enough for everyone to hear, about his fishing boat *Stella* that had come ashore during the storm. "Yup, standing high and dry with much of her hull damaged." Listening to hear what Freddy had to say, the room grew still. "She was mostly destroyed in the storm. She'll be scuttled. I'll have to find another boat before the spring fishing season. Keep your eyes and ears open for me." Everyone nodded.

Someone called out, "You'll have the best boat in the fleet by spring." There were a few chuckles. Davy Souza began talking about the U.S. Coast Guard Cutter that broke loose from its mooring and came up against the pilings of Nonny's wharf. "The boat was smashed to pieces, blew apart like matchsticks. It took out a large section of the wharf as well." He explained that a trap-shed used to store fishing gear was gone and would have to be rebuilt. "The shanty will most likely be built from the scraps washed up along the beach, if Nonny can find enough."

At the tip of Cape Cod the citizens of Provincetown suffered only flooded basements, small skiffs and dories destroyed, some found hundreds of feet from where they'd been left. The town had not suffered much damage. Provincetown felt blessed because they didn't lose a single person. There was a sense of relief, a fragile peace, and giving thanks came naturally to these men who worked the sea. Holding the Fishermen's Ball was their way of celebrating their good fortune while recognizing the needs of others. But Manny was not smiling tonight. He didn't wish to share his gloomy thoughts with the men round the tables. He wasn't listening to the conversation about the ball, the storm or other banter about the town. He was thinking about the men in the room. He knew them to be honest, helpful, and hard working, not the kind of men to be involved in murder.

Frank Rosa rose from his seat. "There is coffee on the burner and pumpkin bread on the back table, if anyone's interested." The men around the room began standing and stretching their bodies. Frank continued, "The town did a good job pushing and shoveling all the sand off the front street after the storm. My house and shop looked like it was sitting in the middle of a sand dune. All I needed was a palm tree and I could sell lemonade to the tourists this summer." He laughed.

Sivert Benson turned the conversation. "I read that over two thousand boats were lost. Fifty thousand homes and businesses destroyed, millions of dollars in damages. Not to mention the six hundred people who lost their lives. And me in the insurance business." He shook his head, "People will rebuild, but it will take months, maybe years, and that's the lucky ones who can afford to. It's a mess."

Jimmy-the-fish-buyer was an optimistic man, but not tonight. He spoke rapidly, "The news on the radio is dark. But we've much to be thankful for. We all know a few of the local boats had damage: the *Elmer S.* and the *Viola D.* As Freddy Salvador said, the *Stella* will be scraped, but most of the boats are back out fishing and doing pretty good." Jimmy had a short, stocky frame that was becoming rounder in the belly now that he did little physical labor. He had reached an age and point in life when hard work was no longer required of

111

him. But he still knew what was going on around the wharfs. "I understand John Worthington of Pond Village Cold Storage lost his boat the *Bocage* when it smashed on shore in North Truro. We'll do what we can to help." The men in the room began to brake into small groups.

Jimmy the-fish-buyer sat down next to Manny. Jimmy usually had a cigar in his mouth and a Portuguese cap on his head, but tonight the hat was off and the cigar was in a dish, unlit. He was not one to beat around the bush. He leaned in as he turned to Manny. His voice was hushed, "What's the news on the boy, Manny?"

Manny's eyes narrowed. He rubbed his hand over his scratchy jaw, shook his head as if to shake out bad thoughts. He answered, "The chief is looking for a ship that arrived in town around October 16. That's the day we found him. He wants to know how he arrived and why he came here. It might have something to do with his death." The death was not spoken of openly, not sensationalized in the local paper, but most of the men in the room knew he had died mysteriously from a stab wound in his chest. Rumors spread rapidly across the small town like fire on wind.

"I met the man twice." Jimmy said. "I was told he was a good crewman and I helped him get a job on the *Annabella R.* Why? What's Crowley thinking?"

"There aren't many leads and he doesn't tell me much." Manny didn't want to talk about Alonzo, but he added, "He was just twenty-four years old, for heaven sake, too young to die." He'd been wrestling with the idea that trouble had followed Alonzo to Provincetown. "I can't imagine anyone from town wanting to murder him. He was here for such a short time."

Jimmy picked up his cigar, pointing it toward Manny. "Long enough to make an enemy." His words were too loud. He lowered his voice. "I lent him some money, but that's another story." The fish buyer changed the subject. "There are too many bad things going on in the world, especially in Europe." The Munich Pact signed by Italy, France and Britain gave Czechoslovakia to Germany. The fish buyer continued, "My wife has relatives there. They're calling it a policy of appeasement, trying to maintain peace after Germany annexed Austria." He stood and pulled on his overcoat.

Jimmy wasn't afraid of anything or anyone. The fish buyer had grown up poor, eating fish and potatoes all his life. He began working on fishing boats at the age of twelve. He had seen men lost in storms, boats that didn't return to port. He fished for twenty-five years on different vessels, in all kinds of weather, with all kinds of men. There is an expression: *you can take the man out of the sea, but you can't take the sea out of the man*, and that explained *Jimmy-the-fish-buyer*.

With coffee cups in hand Big Billy Segura and Carlos Suvera stepped up to the table to get a piece of pumpkin bread. "Good cake," Carlos said as he looked at Jimmy. "I'm hoping to expand my trucking business. I don't like running an empty truck back to the city. I don't like stepping on toes, either, so I hope you won't take it personal that I've asked a few of the captains for their business?" The men stood in a semicircle waiting to see what Jimmy would have to say.

Jimmy was quick to answer, "The fishermen can do as they like. If you're paying more than I can, well, I'll not stand in your way. Business is business, there's enough to go around." Jimmy felt that most of the men that sold their fish to him would stay. They were a loyal group. He understood how business worked and he wasn't against competition. As the middleman between the boats and the stores, Jimmy had thirty men working for him.

Fish from fifteen different boats unloaded at Jimmy's building on any given day of the week. There were other fish buyers and truckers like him scattered around the waterfront, but his outfit was a little bigger. In winter he hired men to cut blocks of ice from Clapper's Pond, sliding them out of the woods on rolling poles, using sleds and horses. He stored the blocks wrapped in straw inside sheds on the outskirts

114

of town until the warm months when he sold them at a good profit. The ice went to the homes that had no electricity, to the restaurants, and to a few of the fishing boats. His main income came from fish. The ice was a bonus. He'd been born and raised in Provincetown and was trusted by those who knew him. The word around town was that he would help friends and relatives when the going got tough, lending a helping hand, or lending a few dollars until payday. Jimmy drove a Packard, had a home on the hill just north of town, and his wife wore a seal-fur coat in winter. He gave a nod of his head and walked away. Billy and Carlos went back to the corner table with cake and coffee in their hands.

Manny followed the fish buyer back to the table on the opposite side of the room. When Manny sat down next to him, Jimmy said in a quiet voice, "On that other business, I'll ask around. Maybe one of the men will remember something about a boat coming to town in late October. Anything I can do, just ask."

Manny thanked him and then said, "Will it hurt your business to have more men trucking fish? That could have an affect on your bottom line."

Jimmy shook his head. "Naw, I've been thinking about spending more time next to the wood stove, at home with the misses. I'm getting too old to keep up with all the work."

Manny smiled. "Not you, you'll be down on the wharf at dawn until you can no longer climb the stairs, and that won't be for fifty or more years." The two men were laughing when the other advertising committee members returned to the table.

They discussed how the proceeds from the Fishermen's Ball should be divided. The four men agreed that the whole association would vote and it could be decided after a final tally, after the ball. Sivert interjected, "In the meanwhile the Linen Thread Company of Boston and Gloucester has sent a check for $200.00. They supply much of the netting, manila and tarred lines to the fishing fleet. I think we should give them a cover page. And on the other side of the booklet we have the Hathaway Oil Co. They sent a donation of $200.00 as well." The other three men nodded approval. Sivert Benson made a few more suggestions and then the meeting broke up.

It was past nine o'clock when Manny arrived home. Eleanor was awake, in a flannel nightgown, under heavy blankets, reading Marjorie Rawlings' new book *The Yearling*. Manny climbed into bed. She put the book aside, "Burr, your feet are like ice." And then in a softer voice, "I'm worried about Mary. We need to talk to her, together, in the morning. She was keeping something." Eleanor whispered. "Under her mattress, a coin."

It had been a long day and Manny wanted to sleep. "All right, we'll talk in the morning. Good night Eleanor." He was thinking about Mary saving money. She could open a bank account, but it could wait until morning. He felt exhausted. Turning on his side, he was asleep within minutes.

Chapter 11

The Diogo home came to life at seven o'clock during the darker winter months. The girls were reluctant to leave their warm beds. On this particular morning the family sat with bowls of oatmeal, hot applesauce, milk, and tea at their usual time. The daughters were dressed for school and as they finished the meal Eleanor said, "Mary, please stay behind today. Emily and Juliana, you two will be walking with Helen Roger's daughters. I spoke to Mrs. Rogers yesterday, you'll meet them across the street." Everyone nodded and the talk returned to the Christmas holidays. Manny sat sipping coffee, perusing the paper.

Mary was quiet until her sisters left for school and then she asked, "Why did you want me to stay behind?"

Eleanor folded her dishtowel and turned to face her daughter, "I found this coin while cleaning." She opened her hand. "I'd like you to show it to your father. And I'd like you to explain how it came to be under your mattress." There was a neutral expression on both parents' faces. They waited for her to speak.

Mary opened her mouth to say something but nothing came out. She looked at her mother. Her father seemed mystified. She said, "You don't understand. It's mine. I didn't do anything wrong." Mary blurted out the words, blushed, and turned her head away from her parents.

"I didn't say you had done something wrong." Her mother spoke gently. "I think this is a German coin and your father needs to see it." The coin in her hand lay like a jewel, bright with the unmistakable patina of gold.

Manny took it, felt the weight in his palm. He thought it might have value or great significance but couldn't think how. The metal seemed to have its own heat. There was a date, 1894, and the words Kaiser Wilhelm II Deutscher, and then some numbers. All three looked at the coin. Then both parents looked at her, waiting. Manny spoke first. "Mary, please tell us how you came to have this." He took a deep breath. There was softness about him when he talked to his daughters. They all knew he was a pushover when it came to getting on his good side. He said, "This is

German, gold, and probably worth quite a bit of money."

"He gave it to me." Mary said tentatively. Her eyes filled with tears. Eleanor put her arm around her waiting for her to continue. "Alonzo said it was a gift to me. That it was because he loved me." Her parents shared a look, but said nothing. Mary went on, "He wanted to marry me when I finished secretarial school." The tears fell in large drops landing on her folded arms.

Manny wanted to ask how long this had been going on, but instead asked, "Do you know where Alonzo got the coin? This may be important." He had not told his daughter how Alonzo had died. The news in the paper only said that his body had been found on the beach next to the cold storage wharf and most people thought he fell and drown. Only a few knew the truth, and these men did not wish to frighten their wives and daughters or to spread rumors. Manny asked his daughter, "Please Mary. We're not angry. I'd just like you to tell us about this coin. What did he tell you about it?"

Their daughter straightened her shoulders, raised her chin and looked directly at her father. Her voice was whispered, "We met after school out near the cemetery. Emily and Juliana never came with me. I told them I was studying." She looked into her father's eyes. "We went for walks." Mary sat at the kitchen table with her arms wrapped tightly around herself like a leaf on a still pond waiting to be blown in any direction. "We walked into town, sometimes we walked on the beach on the west end, and sometimes went to one of the fish shacks, just to sit and talk."

Manny's first reaction was a blinding fear that his daughter might have had relations, but he did not fuel the fire with his thoughts. He held his breath, waiting to hear the rest. She looked at him with opened eyes. "Nothing happened. We held hands. He said he would wait for me to finish my schooling."

Manny let out his breath audibly, wanting to believe her.

"Papa," she said, "We only met a few times. We didn't do anything bad."

"Oh, Sweetheart." He spoke in a soft voice. "I only need to know where this coin came from." This was new territory for him. He felt heat come into his cheeks and was suddenly faced with the idea that his little girl was growing up. But before he could face that fact or say anything else, she jumped to her feet.

"I can't tell you," she yelled as she ran out of the room. Her footsteps going up the stairs seemed to shake the house as well the nerves of her parents. Mary had made up her mind to keep Alonzo's secret. She would not tell that he took the coin from the pocket of the first mate when he jumped from the ship. She would not reveal his secrets. Mary came down the stairs ten minutes later, her face was washed, hair brushed, "I'm going to school." Neither parent tried to stop her.

They sat at the table sipping cold coffee, the coin still on the table between them. "This shouldn't be such a surprise to us. I think we both knew something was going on with her." Eleanor touched his hand. They sat without speaking for some minutes.

Manny heard the surf pounding against the sand outside their kitchen. He picked up the coin. "I think I'll see what James thinks of this." He left the kitchen holding the coin as if he were afraid to put it down or into his pocket. After a few minutes the bell above the door tingled as Manny closed the shop and walked into town.

Ten minutes later Manny opened the door to the police chief's office. Crowley was seated behind his desk and surprise showed on his face. "Manny," he said, looking at his long time friend, "What can I do for you?"

The shopkeeper held out his hand, palm up. The chief stood, leaned in, and then came around the desk to get a better look. Manny said, "Mary had this. It came from Alonzo."

Chief Crowley looked at the coin as he said, "I've been in touch with the state police. The body has gone to Pocasset, to the medical examiner's office. There's a detective in Boston I have spoken with about Alonzo.

I'll run this by him." He took the coin, bouncing it lightly, weighing it in his palm, and then placing it on his desk in front of him. "Do you mind if I keep this for a while? I'll give you a receipt." Manny nodded and the police chief continued, "Anything to do with Alonzo could be helpful." He wrote out a piece of paper describing the coin and handed it to Manny. The next question hung in the air. Neither spoke while they thought about the gold that lay before them. "He gave this to Mary?" The chief asked. Manny nodded yes. The two men looked at each other with a mix of concern and commitment. "I'm curious; do you know where he got it?"

Manny shook his head, "No."

The two men talked about varying possibilities. The chief said, "He was in town for less than two months. Could be enough time to have made friends and enemies. I'd like to know who they were and what kind of man this Alonzo was." Both men stood. Manny had his hand on the doorknob when the policeman added, "Sorry Manny, but I'll need to talk to Mary again. We'll get to the bottom of this. Give Eleanor my best and tell her not to worry. I'll see you both soon."

Manny returned home via the beach through the kitchen. The tide was out. He took a moment to survey the poles holding the bulkhead. They also held up the small wharf that jutted into the bay from his property.

He stared briefly at the building that was his home, glanced at the side of the building where they had found Alonzo and then hurried up the stairs.

Eleanor was rubbing clothing on a washboard at the kitchen sink when he walked in. Taking off his coat, he said, "James is in contact with his friends in Boston. He said to tell Mary that he would give the coin back once they were through with it. He gave me a receipt." Eleanor sensed that there was more. She dried her hands. There was a brief hug.

Manny said, "He's going to need to speak with Mary again. James said a couple of fishermen remember a trawler that appeared in the harbor during an October gale. He thinks it may have brought Alonzo to town." His wife was quiet. "He doesn't believe he walked all the way from Boston and somehow managed to make it to our doorstep. Coming by water makes more sense."

"James also said that it might not be connected to Alonzo's death. He is looking into reports that a vessel came into the harbor at the end of October. It didn't have any nets in the rigging or on deck, and there were men walking around smoking cigarettes. He's not sure it has anything to do with the boy. So far no one remembers the name. The chief will check it out." Manny looked at his wife, "James said for us not to worry."

She relaxed her shoulders, softening, and then leaning into Manny. She said, "Keep the closed sign in the window and come upstairs, I need to feel you close to me." The closed sign stayed in the window well into the afternoon.

Manny was taking inventory in the shop and Eleanor was browning a chicken for a stew that would be served with carrots and dumplings when the girls came in from school. They each took an apple and headed up the stairs. There was no talk about coins. Eleanor looked out her kitchen window. Steel grey clouds lay across her view. This had been a hard winter, but her family was getting used to the idea that death was a part of life. With the girls getting older and the business was doing well she felt she had no reason to worry.

"It's time the family moved into the twentieth century." Eleanor said. They had discussed the idea of getting rid of the icebox. She complained about the melting, water sometimes spilling over onto the hall floor and food spoiling in summer if it wasn't eaten right away. A picture in the newspaper of a new Westinghouse refrigerator lay open on the table. Manny had told her that it looked like next year they would pay off the mortgage and then they could do a bit of upgrading.

Progress could be seen around the sleepy town on the sandy tip of the cape. A new Oldsmobile was selling at Duarte Motors for $850. There were more cars appearing on the streets with every passing day. New houses had been built along Bradford Street and people were smiling. Eleanor came in from the store one afternoon to tell her husband that their neighbor Herman Dutra just gave his wife a bright yellow Chevy convertible as a wedding present. She said, "He works for Joe Duarte as a mechanic, you know who I mean." The conversations were meant to keep thoughts of death away from their kitchen table.

Alonzo died on December 6th and on December 14th a gale with sixty knots of wind, blowing first from the north and then from the south, pounded the shoreline. Manny tucked the paper behind him and said, "That storm on the fourteenth took the Atlantic Coast Fisheries building right off its foundations." The head of the house had everyone's attention that night at supper. "The newspaper said that fishermen from town got together with farmers from Truro. Men from both towns brought in five teams of horses to help pull their weir-nets from the fish-house that fell into the water."

The girls were listening. "They were able to salvage $20,000 worth of nets. You know that's enough to send Mary's whole graduating class to Harvard University next year. Manuel told his family that Manuel Gracie at the Highland Coast Guard Station said the fishermen worked through the night to save the equipment. "The building was a total loss. There's a picture of it here in the *Advocate*." The building lay on its side, off its foundation of poles, with debris littered all along the beachfront. "Some of the planks and wood washed up right in front of our bulkhead, but they saved those nets. Good for them." Around the Diogo table news of death was kept at bay as the head of the house chose what to repeat to his daughters.

The destruction from the hurricane remained in the news three months later, but Manny did not share with his family much of what was published. Over five hundred bodies had been recovered, two hundred-seven from along the Rhode Island coast. The newspaper reported that there was more damage done in New England than from the 1906 San Francisco earthquake. Along with the shock and sadness, the citizens of Provincetown felt a sense of optimism and national pride when the U.S. Navy Submarine the 'Cuttlefish' was spotted in Provincetown Harbor. Manny spoke to his family about national pride and the defense of our shores. The news of war in Asia, unrest in Europe and the death of Alonzo were not discussed around the dinner table.

There was a hiatus in meetings for the Fishermen's Ball during the weeks leading up to Christmas, giving Manny time to restock his shelves, read the paper, and think. As 1938 came to an end there would be celebrations for the New Year and then the big dance on January 19. Manny had to admit he was looking forward to it. His family needed a positive influence.

Chapter 12

It had been three weeks since Alonzo was found on the beach. Mary Diogo thought she knew and loved the dead man. Davy Souza was jealous and hated him. Manny wished that he'd never stopped at their door. Eleanor's heart ached for the loss of life and Chief Crowley saw the darkest side of it. The trail left in Alonzo's wake seemed like a tsunami.

It took constant effort to push the daydreams of Alonzo from Mary's mind and replace them with the unquestionable truth of his death. She was yearning for things beyond her reach. Thoughts of the strong arms that she would never feel again caused her to suddenly leave a room or to walk away from the group of girls who tried surrounding her with their friendship. Even now, like a bad dream, she saw her life as if looking through a magnifying glass. She felt like she was underwater most of the time. School was a solace. Mrs. Francis, the English teacher was now speaking about the virtue of Mr. Shakespeare and what he had to teach us about human nature, but Mary was not listening. She was remembering the words, the touch and the feelings that had been awakened deep inside her. She was afraid she might forget those feelings.

Mary and Alonzo met the first time by accident. She admitted to herself that she had been wishing she could see him again. Sometimes the dream is better than the reality, but on that day Mary's reality became her dream. They each had a reason to be on the west end of town on the third day of November. Mary was meeting her friend Susan so that the two could study for the exams. She was deep in thought when out of the blue Alonzo bumped past her on his way around the corner of Court Street and Commercial. He was in a hurry to pass and said, "Excuse me." They nodded their heads and looked at each other. They both smiled. Her heart leaped.

"Hi. I'm just coming from the Captain's home. We walk, yes? I walk with you." It was a question and a statement. He asked about her family. They had been so generous to him. He offered to carry her small bag, but she said it wasn't a problem. "The cold weather is coming, I think." It was a blustery day just a week after he'd left their home.

"Yes. It is," she answered, pulling herself into her wool coat.

They slowed their pace, neither aware of the shops, the wind, or the views of the harbor as they walked. "I would like to thank you again," he said.

They continued talking about friends, boats, fishing, school, the Fishermen's Ball, the Azorean Islands, and their family until they realized they had reached the end of Commercial Street. They stopped to look out across the vast marshlands with the sun beginning its winter display of color; the sky was enveloped in gold and purple. He reached for her hand, but she turned away and laughed about how they had completely lost track of time.

"Do you meet your friend everyday to study?" He asked as they walked back toward the town center. "Most days we are in from fishing by four o'clock, we could talk again. Could I buy you a hot chocolate before going home?" His words to her felt like a spring zephyr that had blown in from the south, a rising swell, warming her.

For a moment she could not speak. She dipped her head, brought her chin toward her right shoulder, and looked him in the eyes. She said, "We could meet at Perry's Market. They have hot chocolate and it's on my way home from Susan's house. Can you be there at four, tomorrow?" Mary would spend time studying at her friend's home on West Vine Street and she would tell Susan that she had to go home early. She wasn't expected until five o'clock and maybe she could find a reason for coming home late.

"I see you tomorrow," Alonzo's singing voice was hanging in the air as he walked away, up Court Street toward his room at the Bradford Street Inn. Mary turned toward home. She was aware of a strange giddy feeling in her chest. She knew her mother rarely ventured passed the center of town. Her shopping was done at the First National Store on the east side of Railroad Wharf. Her father stayed close to his shop or had meetings at the town hall. She would meet Alonzo on the west side of town, away from her family. The voice inside her told her that she was playing with fire. There was an element of danger to the way she was feeling, but she didn't want to discuss Alonzo with anyone. Like a treasure or gift that she'd given to herself she would not mention the encounter to anyone, especially her parents who she knew would not approve.

Memories and dreams seemed to blend with her days after Alonzo was gone. She remembered an afternoon when they had walked out to Fishermen's Wharf and stood in the lee of the building, protected from the strong north winds that constantly battered the coast. He had leaned against her, put his cheek next to her and spoke of how sweet she smelled, like the lavender that grew in his mother's yard in San Miguel. Then he took her hand and held her there next to the building. He told her of his childhood and of his mother's mother who lived to be one hundred years old. "It was a simple life, yes," he said. "We were poor, very poor. That is why I had to leave. And I am happy that I found you." Their lips met in a brief yet tender kiss. The sensations unnerved her, sucking her in and she was afraid she could not stop, but Alonzo was a gentleman. "We have plenty of time," he said, "*Bom*, is good."

During the next meeting, bundled in woolens, they walked along the beach on the shore of Provincetown Harbor, ignoring the cold and wind. Alonzo told Mary about the boats that he had worked on since he'd left his home almost four years ago. His English was sometimes nonexistent as he searched for words, but like a guessing game they found communicating fun. He told her that he had fished for a time from Marseille, France, telling Mary about the great castle of Monte-Cristo that sits on an island in the Gulf of Leon. And the beautiful Notre-Dam de la Garde with mosaics of gold and glass of many colors that was built on the highest hill in 1524 to protect the city. "It is now a Basilica."

Four months ago he signed on as crew with a freighter bound for the West Indies. They laughed at the ship's name, *The Zuiderdijk*. He had said it with a Portuguese accent and Mary had tried to pronounce it, but could not. Alonzo told her that the ship had taken refuge in Provincetown Harbor because of a northeast gale. Alonzo said, "I had to get off that ship. The captain was drunk all the time. Strange things had happened, things I didn't like. While we were in Kingston, in the Bahamas, four men were taken on as crew, but they never left their cabin. I heard one speaking German." The talk on the radio has been about war and unrest in Poland. He did not want to frighten Mary so he said no more about the ship or its cargo.

"You did the right thing by leaving," Mary replied. "I'm glad you're here." Her white teeth gleamed in a big smile. Alonzo saw sensuality in the smile. He wanted her as any man would.

When they met for the third time they walked to the far end of town, stopping on the way back next to a fish shed. He gently put his arm over her shoulder and said, "When you go away to school in the fall, how far is it? Will you come home? I can work hard. I am saving money." He had a few dollars left over at the end of each week. He told her that he liked his job and felt he could grow roots in this community. He had met other Portuguese men who left the old country for reasons similar to his own: no work, no money and no incentive. They sat together on unopened barrels inside a shack at the end of Taves wharf. The boatyard was deserted. The *Alice J* was hauled out of water on the rails, but the main shop was locked. They were alone. Looking out the door of the tiny space, thighs touching, Alonzo had placed his hand on hers and said, "Mary, I hope when you are done with school," he hesitated, "we can be married." She didn't speak.

A cold wind whistled past the doorway that faced the water. The area was deserted except for the wooden ladders, staging, and boat hauling equipment that lay piled alongside the main boat shop. Buckets that had once held paint were stacked in a haphazard pile at the side alley. Lumber was stacked waiting to be shaped to fit some piece of a boat. Mary listened to the water lapping against the pilings as it made its way steadily up the sand with the incoming tide. Surprised by his words, she answered, "I don't know what to say." This time she did not resist his lips on hers, nor the caresses of his hands as they slid along her legs still wrapped in woolen stockings.

When Mary arrived home the house was filled with warmth and steam. A pot with spaghetti noodles was boiling on the wood stove and her mother was wiping her hands on the apron she always wore while cooking. "There you are. I thought I was going to have to send out a search party. It gets dark early these days." Her mother glanced up from the pan. "Go upstairs and change, get ready for supper. Your sisters may need help." Eleanor did not notice the flush on her daughter's face, the cold brought rosy cheeks to all her daughters. Mary quickly made for the stairs, mumbling about spending time with Teresa Perry. Her sisters would be too worried about their own difficulties to care about what was happening in her life.

She had felt things were moving forward quickly, but there was also a need to give something to the man who found his new life at their home. She wanted to care for him like a found puppy, to hold him. There were other feelings just below the surface, feelings that she would not have been able to describe if anyone had asked and she was grateful that no one did. They met in secret, but now something in her was changing.

She began feeling guilty and nervous after what happened on a sunny Sunday morning just before Thanksgiving. Davy Souza looked across the isle at St. Peter's Church and caught her eyes. He smiled his usual happy smile and Mary began to return the smile as friends and neighbors do, but then she turned, and saw Alonzo. The look spoke volumes. Her face changed. It flamed to something like embarrassment or shame. Davy looked from her to Alonzo and then he looked away. He knew. And she knew that he did. There was an awkward moment when Alonzo greeted the Diogos as they walked up the aisle. Mary kept her head down hoping no one noticed her blush. In church that Sunday Mary saw the confusion, anger and sadness in Davy's eyes. He spoke her name: "Mary" and then he fled down the aisle.

Mary and Alonzo continued to meet on Franklin Street, away from the center of town. They hid in the shed at the boat yard after work hours, talking about friends, family and fishing. They began necking, hot passionate kisses, breathing rapidly, wanting more. Mary was hoping their relationship could remain unchanged. As Edmund Spencer (1552-1599) said "*So let us love, dear Love, like as we ought, -Love is the lesson which the*

Lord us taught." Love is one of nature's mighty laws and so their relationship would evolve.

His hands found their way to her breasts and lately he'd taken to placing her hand on his erection. He didn't pressure her for sex, but there was no doubt that things were heating up, and it frightened Mary. One Friday at twilight she had asked him to stop when his hand slid under her skirt and tore at her underpants. Breathless he breathed into her neck, *"Sim*, yes. *O que devo fazer*? What am I to do?"

She stood up, began rearranging her clothing, wanting to leave. He told her that he would wait. They both knew it was only a matter of time before Mary would not be able to stop him and she was afraid she would not want to. Mary was also confused by the thoughts of her parents. What would they say if she told them she was seeing Alonzo. Why did she feel guilty and shameful as if she were doing something wrong? Love couldn't be wrong, could it? Their relationship was growing. She had kept their meetings secret, hidden. There would be consequences if the truth came out. Her father would be furious. Her mother would fret, worrying about her future. And her friend Davy was hurting. She had seen the look on his face and felt a stab of regret. But she kept silent.

Mary and Alonzo met in front of Perry's Market on the west end of town. They hurried to the boatyard shed, where Alonzo pulled at her, drawing her closer, kissing her. Unexpectedly one afternoon he turned her hand up and placed a large yellow-gold coin into her palm. He said, "Keep this for us. To show I am serious."

Surprised, Mary responded in a whisper, "Alonzo, What is this? It's beautiful." She looked at his unshaven face. He seemed older, his eyes tired, and his smile barely visible. "Where did this come from?"

He lowered his head. "The coin is my payment for the work I did on the ship." He pulled her close, kissing her cheek and neck. She stiffened as his hands pulled at her coat, pushing it open to roam under her sweater. He whispered, "I know I can trust you." Lifting her chin to meet his eyes Mary saw something new in them. They hardened. She was frightened and pulled away.

He said, *"Fazer para mim favor."* It was a favor, a promise. "Don't tell anyone about the coin, not your *madra* or *papa*, no one." His voice was firm. Mary frowned. Alonzo continued, "It is just for us, *meu amor.*" He pulled her to him. He was strong. His body was hard and her body softened against him. He said, "Please, keep the coin. *Sim?* Yes?"

Her face was burning, knees shaking when she pulled away. The young woman was suddenly confused. "Yes Alonzo, I'll keep it safe, but why a secret? Can't I show this to my mother?" He told her that he didn't want to lose her. He said that her parents would ask questions that he couldn't answer. "I don't want you to say anything to your parents until after you graduate from school. Do you understand? *Compreendido*?"

She did. She held the coin tightly in her hand while he closed the door to the shed. They walked up the alley turning right onto Commercial Street and just before they parted, Alonzo stopped and said, "Mary, I need to tell you something." She looked at him and he continued, "I took the coin before I left the ship."

"You mean you stole this? Take it back. I don't want it." The words had a sharp edge and she didn't like the way she was feeling.

"I'm sorry," he said. He explained in his broken English that the coin was his pay, owed to him. They stopped walking. "Please Mary. I can't return it."

She hesitated, "All right, I'll keep the coin safe, Alonzo. It will be our secret." They walked back to the center of town together. Alonzo told her he would be fishing long hours, out of his bed at three o'clock in the morning and not back until after sunset. Darkness came early and left late. Mary was busy with school.

The last time she saw Alonzo was the night of December 4 when he came to see her at her home and was greeted by her father who frowned, but then left them alone. Alonzo told her he had to go away. He didn't know for how long. She remembered how his eyes darted around. He kept pushing his hair back with a nervous hand and looking towards the door. "Don't worry, just for a short while." And then he was gone.

And now, sitting in Mrs. Francis's English class, she came back to the reality that drew her away from daydreams and memories of love, lust, and loss.

Chapter 13

Manny closed the shop after lunch and walked the three blocks to Chief Crowley's office. Patrolman Lewis was at his desk when he opened the door. The new recruit had come straight from the Massachusetts Police Academy just three months ago. He stood up and nodded when Manny entered. "The chief's in his office. I'll tell him you're here." Manny kept walking, straight into the chief's office, slumping into the chair. He said, "I need to talk to you. Do you have a minute?"

"Of course Manny, always glad to see you." The Chief looked over Manny's shoulder and nodded at patrolman Lewis. "Close the door on your way out, Thomas." When they were alone, the chief looked at Manny and said, "You look tired."

"I didn't plan on spending my holidays worrying about things I don't understand. What have you learned about this awful business?" Manny asked.

Crowley let out a breath like he was blowing out a candle. "We're working on it." He paused. "I've a question for you." He looked into Manny's eyes, "Did you know that Davy Souza and Alonzo had a fight in front of the bowling alley, just a few days before he died?" Manny raised his eyebrows and shook his head.

The chief continued. "From what I've heard it wasn't nice. Hot words, punches thrown, and blood spilled."

Manny sat up straight. He coughed, shook his head. "You're not suggesting that Davy Souza had anything to do with Alonzo's death, are you?" Steam hissed somewhere overhead as Manny continued, "Even if he got into it a bit with Alonzo, doesn't mean he killed him." The shopkeeper felt he could be honest with his old friend. "You know as well as I do that fights sometimes happen around the wharf." The police chief was about to speak when Manny interrupted, "Davy's been known to have a temper, but I've never thought of Davy as being violent. In fact just the opposite." His eyebrows came together and his voice held anger. "He's practically family. What the hell are you thinking?"

"Let's leave Davy to me. I'll talk to him and get to the bottom of this." The Chief paused and then reluctantly added, "I've talked to everyone who knew Alonzo, men around the wharfs, the woman who runs the boarding house where he lived and the crewmen he worked with. No one seems to know much about the fellow. He kept to himself." The policeman hesitated, not wanting to open a delicate subject, but he had no choice. "I'm sorry Manny, but I need to talk with Mary again. She talked to the man." The chief spoke quietly to his long time friend. He knew that Manny was protective of his girls. "Even the smallest detail could help."

The chief thought about his friendship with Manny and Eleanor. They'd gone to the Center School together, graduated high school together. James Crowley had gone to Manny and Eleanor's wedding. He'd been away in the Army when he'd received a card telling him that a baby girl was born and they had named her Mary. He had relinquished any jealousy that penetrated his heart, glad for his friends, but this was murder and the chief had to put his feelings for his friends aside when it came to finding the truth.

Manny Diogo interrupted the chief's thoughts. "I'd protect my family with my life." He said, "James, I need you to be honest with me here. Is Mary in any danger?"

The chief took a sip of cold coffee, swallowed hard, and then said, "Let me put it this way, there is much here we don't understand." The two friends sat quietly. Manny watched James shuffle some papers. The policeman said, "Davy has a crush on Mary, you must know that. That along with the fight at the pool hall, maybe things got out of hand."

Manny told the chief that he'd suspected that Davy was infatuated with his daughter for about a year. "Davy had been coming to his store weekly, but then, just after Thanksgiving, he'd stopped coming in altogether." Manny watched Crowley make a note on his pad.

The chief looked up and said, "It was my understanding that Davy gave Alonzo a job on his boat, but then Alonzo moved to another boat, the *Annabella R.*" They both knew that crewmen often worked one boat then another, where help is needed. The police chief continued, "We're putting together a picture of Alonzo, but there is still so much we don't know about him." The police chief hesitated, hoping his friend was already aware of the situation. "Mary was seen a number of times with Alonzo." He looked at Manny. "This fight between Davy and Alonzo, well honestly, it doesn't look good." The chief looked directly into Manny's eyes. "Maybe Davy was jealous. I don't think he would harm Mary." Both men thought about what young love can be like. The policeman added, "We don't know what Davy may have done in a burst of anger. Add in a bit of firewater and frustration," The police chief gave his head a twist and pulled on his mustache, "It can lead to an explosion."

Manny didn't like what he was hearing. He spoke in defense of Davy. "Then again, James, like you said, we don't know everything about Alonzo either. What about the coin? He may have been running from someone when he came to town. What about the ship? Seems to me we are jumping to conclusions." He scowled as he thought again about Alonzo. "The man brought trouble with him. From the first day he washed up at my door I've had a bad feeling about him." Manny stood up abruptly.

Chief Crowley looked at his friend. "This is just between you and me, Manny. I know you like Davy, we all do, but I need to look at this with unbiased eyes. I'll know more in a couple of days. I'm meeting with a detective from Boston." He didn't tell his friend that he planned to search Davy's room, his workshop in his backyard and the boat when they could get it from the mooring to the pier.

The room was growing hot. The police chief removed his jacket and said, "Seems Davy's been doing a bit of drinking at the pool hall." The chief pulled his shoulders back, "I'm not taking any chances. I don't want you to worry, just be aware. And please leave this to the police."

Manny was at the door. "Thanks. But, I think you're wrong about Davy. Let me know if anything develops. I'll keep a close eye on my family." There was tension in Manny's voice, "I'm on my way to the Legion Hall. We've got the ball pretty much wrapped up. You're coming, right?"

The chief stood, nodding in the affirmative, "Of course. I'll be in touch. Please don't worry, Mary is safe and I'll be talking to Davy."

When Manny left the police department he crossed Commercial Street and took the wooden steps on the outside of the building to the second floor hall of the Legion Hall where a meeting for the big dance was being held. The open room was filled with men. He spotted Jimmy-the-fish-buyer, Frank the barber and Sivert Benson at the corner table in the back of the room. At another table near the front of the room sat, Billy Segura, Billy King and Carlos Suvera with their heads together in conversation. At other tables sat bankers, hotel managers, the school superintendent, and fishermen. Manny didn't see Davy Souza in the smoke filled room. He made his way passed tables greeting some of the men. "Evening, Manny," Big Billy said. "Looks like we've got ourselves a shindig."

Manny stopped at their table giving Billy time to continue, "Hey did you see there was a Navy submarine in the harbor last week, a new S type. Named *Salmon*, like the fish. Good name for it, don't ya think." He chuckled. "I hear that its captain, Charles Foster is staying in town. There's going to be a

143

ceremony when he takes command of the sub, right here in Provincetown. That's something."

Manny smiled, "Yeah, I heard." He nodded to the other two men and moved to the back of the room to work with his committee. He could see the smiles on everyone's faces as he approached the table. The other members of the advertising committee seemed in a good spirits, excited, even jubilant. Jimmy said, "Hey Manny, glad you could make it. We've had plenty of returns and Sivert has put together an accounting. We will be gifting a good deal of money to the American Red Cross with some left over for the Provincetown Ladies Aid Society."

Manny draped his coat on the back of his chair, laid his hat and scarf on the table, and then sat down heavily. There was no enthusiasm in his voice when he spoke. "That's good news." Manny put some papers on the table and the men passed them around. "I've laid out the beginnings of the booklet, to be given out at the door. See what you think." The three other committee members were smiling and nodding their heads in agreement while Manny's head slumped closer to his chest.

Frank Rose said, "The ads look good. I'd like to get a statement from the fishermen who came up with the idea for an overview of their association. We can put it in the front of the booklet. I can ask Captains Russe, Salvador, Lisbon and Macara to write up a page about the Fishermen's Association." The others liked the idea, nodded their heads in agreement, the matter settled.

"I was told by Louie Salvador that there are twenty-nine draggers in the Provincetown Fishermen's Association and they are growing in membership. He said that fishing provides jobs directly to 500 people and indirectly to many more of the town's 4,000 citizens." Frank Rose liked to tell everyone facts. "Whatever good fortune may fall to the lot of the draggermen affects almost every business in this community."

"By the way," Jimmy-the-fish-buyer interrupted, "Speaking of citizens, our friend Davy Souza got his name in the paper again. Have you seen it?" He was smiling. Manny shook his head, thinking about murder and what the chief had just told him.

Manny heard Jimmy answer his own question, "At the last selectmen's meeting, a ruckus broke out between a lobsterman and Davy. The lobsterman was saying that the draggers were targeting their traps, cutting the buoys. Well, Davy got up and defended the fishermen, telling old Willie Brown that no dragger-man would want to get into the lobster gear." Jimmy kept up with the news around town. "At the meeting Davy told the audience that getting traps in their nets, rips up their gear, and when the traps are left on the bottom they continue to catch. He said he didn't want their broken wooden crates rotting on the bottom. And no dragger would target them. It would be losing fishing time, rip nets, and cost money."

Everyone knew that there were problems between the different fishing groups. "Seems like the ocean just isn't big enough." Jimmy continued, "Davy was all fired up that night. It shut Willie's mouth for the time being, because the selectmen are endorsing a petition to the State House that would allow the draggers to keep fishing inside three miles, twenty-four hours a day except during the warmer months of June July August and September when the lobstermen would set their gear." The fish buyer took a breath, and then added, "Sounds good, everyone gets to use the area." He took a puff of his cigar.

Sivert Benson added a comment, "I admire the way the town's fishermen have joined together. They formed a working group that went all the way to Boston last year to the Gardener Auditorium to speak to our state supervisor of marine fisheries, Bernard J. Sheridan and they got the state to act into law protection that would allow the fishermen to continue fishing nights along the back side." The fishermen drew up a petition and it was passed into law. News of their accomplishment was published in all the papers. The insurance salesman continued, "With ideas like this dance they'll keep the government on their side. It won't be easy, because fishing rights might mean something else to the men in Boston. It's a touchy subject."

The talk continued around the table for the next hour. The town seemed to be coming together in a practical as well as a frivolous way. Spirits were high, but Manny didn't feel like talking. He kept quiet and listened. Eventually the men got restless and began stretching, moving around the room, talking in small groups. The food and beverage committee, entertainment committee, and the advertising committee began to mix. Manny and Carlos began talking about the band that was coming all the way from Boston. "It's a big orchestra: trombones, drums, you name it. They have twenty members." Carlos had a smile like the Cheshire cat.

Manny wasn't listening. He was aware of the Old Spice aftershave, but his mind was elsewhere. His attention piqued when he heard Carlos ask, "How's your daughter? I understand she was very upset by the death of that young man. Is there anything I can do to help? I hear they were pretty serious. Was she going to marry the fellow?" Carlos had bought a second truck. He brought cigars and cigarettes, rum and whiskey to town and had started buying, selling, and trading goods as well as shipping fish to New Bedford.

Manny suddenly wished to be home, away from the jubilant talk, the money talk, and talk from Carlos. Manny was tired, but turned and shook the salesman's hand. "She's doing all right. She'll be spending the summer in Boston with her aunt and uncle. Thanks for asking." He turned to get his coat.

They walked across the room together. Carlos said, "I hear Davy Souza was put-out by her being with the immigrant. Can't say as I blame him." Carlos didn't miss a beat, "Well that's what people are saying." Local gossip was normal for a small town, but Manny felt the sting of it just the same.

Manny responded, "You'll have to excuse me, I've got to be getting home." He glared at Carlos and if looks could kill there would be one less on the entertainment committee. The newly arrived salesman had a smirk on his lips. He was a lover of gossip.

The shopkeeper headed for the door. Frank Rosa, the barber followed him out. At the bottom of the stairs the two men paused and looked toward Fishermen's Wharf where a boat was unloading. The vessel was illuminated by a glowing overhead light and the vessels deck lights. It looked like the *Fanny Parnell*, but fog was rolling in, obscuring the surroundings. Frank put his hand on Manny's arm, "Seems there has been some talk about Alonzo and your daughter. Busybody's always asking questions," Frank shook his head. "I nipped that talk right in the bud. I thought you should know."

Manny's face flushed. "Yeah, your right Frank. If everyone would just mind their own business."

Manny hurried away. His breathe, like steam leaving a stopped train, exploding into the cold night air when he reached the other side of the street, thinking about his daughters, his wife, and Alonzo. The shopkeeper was almost home when he caught sight of his own reflection in the glass of John Francis's real estate office. Suddenly out of the darkness behind him, the image of a man appeared, reaching out to him. Manny spun around, sucking in the cold night air. Davy Souza was standing in front of him. Manny felt his neck and face grow hot. "Davy, you startled me. What do you want?" His words echoed in the quiet street.

"I saw you leave the Legion Hall. I just came from the wharf and I wanted to talk to you." His words came in a rush. "It's just that I've been meaning to ask you, I mean I thought I should ask you. What I want to ask you is about Mary. Remember?" Davy was tripping on his words, unsure how to say what was on his mind. He had a fish tied in a string in his hand and made a gesture of raising it.

Manny saved him from speaking further, "If you are asking my permission to take Mary out, the answer is no, it's out the question. Do you understand? No. She doesn't need to be bothered right now. Please just leave her alone. Understand? Not now." Manny turned away, crossed the street, and headed for his shop.

With his head and shoulders slumping toward the ground Davey looked like he'd been run over by a train. He blindly walked away, balling his hands into fists, ready for a fight. Instead of heading for his home on Pearl Street, he turned back toward the center of town and the pool hall.

Chapter 14

Johnny Mott's Bar and Pool Hall was located above the bowling alley on Commercial Street. The room was dark with the smell of smoke and beer, sweat and fish. Davy had found someone to talk to. He was having a couple of beers and shooting pool alongside Charley Holway. Two pool tables were set up in the center of the room. A make shift bar that had no seats occupied the space against the left wall. A few chairs leaned against the other. There were six men in the room.

Davy had been in the poolroom for about an hour. He had a bottle of beer in his hand and was straddling a chair backwards with a waitress leaning over him. They were laughing. The woman ran her hand over his thick hair, down his neck and lingered on his shoulder, while she held a small round tray in the other. Smoke curled from a cigarette hanging between

Davy's lips and his hands curled around the cue stick as if it were holding him up. A light over the center of the table put the rest of the room in dark shadow. Davy was watching Charley aim the cue stick at a triangle of balls in the middle of the table. Charley said, "Can you be quiet for a minute while I break?" Davy had been talking without stopping for thirty minutes.

When Davy complained that he wasn't catching his share of fish, Charley laughed. "There's an old saying that if you ain't been catching, you need to change your luck." Charley had a fun way of looking at things. "Well, I've heard it said that if you need to change your luck, then you should put the boat's engine in reverse and back your boat out of the harbor. It's sure to reverse your luck. You should try it." Charley chuckled and moved the q-stick so that he could rub chalk on the tip.

Davy asked the waitress to get him another beer. She walked away. He had already consumed two bottles of beer. "There's nothing wrong with my luck. Keep the old wives-tales to yourself." Davy tipped up the empty bottle. He said, "It's not fish that keeps me awake at night."

Charley lifted his eyes to Davy and said, "I hear Jimmy-the-fish-buyer loaned Alonzo money before he got himself drowned. I don't know if that's true, but Alonzo wasn't hurting for money. I saw him flash a roll at the bar a couple of weeks ago, enough to choke a horse." Charley looked at the green felt pad and the colorful balls. He said, "And I hear that some hot words were spoken between the two men." Charley gave a chuckle, shook his head from side to side, and then gave the table a tap with the cue stick. "Not like when the two of you went at it, of course." They both remembered the night Alonzo and Davy swapped fisticuffs. Charley remembered pulling Alonzo off of Davy. Charley chuckled, but Davy didn't say a word. Then Charley added, "Yeah, I hear that trouble followed Alonzo wherever he went." He leaned against the wooden wall as Davy took up his position over the table.

The fisherman took aim. Balls collided. They rolled, bouncing against the felt without falling into a pocket. Charley rubbed chalk on the tip of the stick and said, "I don't know if he had any friends, but the crew on the *Annabelle R* liked him. Of course none of those men had their eye on Mary Diogo." Charley grinned. He and Davy had been friends for a number of years. Davy thought Charley looked like a scarecrow. His clothing was loose as if hanging from a clothesline. Charley's family came the hills of Truro where he'd grown up on his parent's farm. He began working on boats in Provincetown when he was eighteen. Now he had his own business delivering fuel to the boats in Provincetown harbor. He was already seeing a profit. When anyone asked him what he did for a living he'd tell them, "Instead of plowing the fields, I'm plying the water, same difference." The two men had been in the same graduating class, Provincetown Class of 1932.

The volume of voices in the background muffled Davy's slurred words. "I just don't understand what Mary saw in him. I thought he was a pig and ugly too."

Davy threw down a shot of whiskey that burned his throat and was about to follow it with a beer when Officer Lewis and Sergeant Santos came into the hall. All talk in the room stopped, the hum of voices gone, as the two uniformed men looked around the room, letting their eyes adjust to the gloom. Davy was looking at the floor. Charley spotted the policemen heading in his direction and put his hands in the air. "I haven't done anything wrong. I swear." He'd spent a few nights sleeping in the holding cell a couple of winters back because he couldn't make it home to the Truro hills in a northeast gale. The two officers looked from Charley to Davy.

The policeman said, "Would you mind coming with us Davy? Chief Crowley wants a few words with you." They didn't expect trouble, but were taught to never underestimate situations, especially when alcohol was involved.

Davy surprised the two officers when he jumped to his feet and yelled, "What's this all about? I'm not doing anything illegal."

"Now calm down. The chief just wants a word. It'll only take a few minutes. Get your coat, we'll give you a ride."

Davy swayed slightly as he stood up, having just come from fishing all day and he wasn't used to alcohol. Officer Lewis reached out, catching him by his arm. Davy pulled away, bringing his arm back as if to swing. At that moment the two policemen each took an arm and held on, leading Davy to the stairs.

"What the hell do you think you're doing?" Davy shouted. "Let go of me." The struggle was useless. The two uniformed men were much larger and although the fisherman was strong and wiry he'd been up for eighteen hours and had had more than his usual one beer. He gave in quickly, pulled himself upright. "All right, all right, I can walk. I'm not that drunk," he said.

Warm water ran through pipes that hung from the ceiling, keeping the town hall warm in winter and the basement overheated. The pipes were heavily painted and exposed, causing everyone to duck their heads when entering. Officer Santos put his hand on Davy's shoulder, "Mind your head." Davy was beginning to sober up as the policemen escorted him down the cement hallway and opened the door that had James Crowley printed across the frosted glass. The chief had removed his sweater and jacket. Davy was overdressed in his heavy coat, wool socks and work boots.

The older man leaned over his desk and said, "Sit down Davy. You're a hard man to find. You seem to be out fishing most of the time. Even in bad weather and your mom says you haven't been home in days." Chief Crowley didn't smile. "I wanted to ask you about that skirmish you had with Alonzo. I want to hear your side of it."

The chief leaned back in his chair. "Take off your coat. I'll get you some coffee." He opened the door and hollered, "Santos, please get me two cups of coffee, black, one with a lot of sugar."

Davy didn't remove his coat even though he felt dizzy from the drink and the heat. He was not used to people telling him what to do. His face was flushed. His skin was beginning to itch from the wool shirt and flannel long johns. He was afraid he might throw up. Neither man said anything for a few minutes. The fisherman wanted to give the police chief a piece of his mind, but he didn't say anything. He needed to go home and lie down. Then the door opened and the patrolman brought in two steaming mugs. "You look a little piqued. Drink this." The chief put the coffee in front of the fisherman and Davy looked up. The chief continued, "Now, tell me about the fight in front of Johnny Mott's."

Davy took a swallow of the hot sweet drink. "What fight? There was no fight." Davy said.

The chief was a patient man. He had heard about the skirmish and would give Davy time to tell his version. Crowley suspected that Davy had good reason to want to see Alonzo gone. He'd spoken to other fishermen and was told that Davy fired Alonzo, but no one knew why. The chief looked across his desk and spoke slowly. "I know all about Mary and Alonzo. And I know all about you." The chief waited. "So let's hear it."

"Keep Mary out of this. All you need to know is that Alonzo was no good. He talked sweet, but he was anything but." Davy's face was ashen. He sipped the hot brew then continued, "I gave him a chance on the boat and yeah, he was a pretty good fisherman, knew his way around the boat. There just wasn't enough fish to keep two crewmen. I let him go." Davy shook his head.

Chief Crowley let Davy take another sip of coffee before saying, "OK, you told him you didn't need another crewman so he had to get off the boat. He must have been pretty upset. Then you ran into him at the pool hall. What did he say that got you so mad?"

Davy lifted his head. "He said things. He said he was glad to be off my boat, he was on a better fishing boat. Plus, the man was a pig."

"So, you fired him. You get into a fight with him, and your telling me it had nothing to do with Mary?"

156

Chief Crowley waited. He picked up a notebook from the desk, turned a page.

"No, it wasn't like that." Davy began to get out of his seat then thought better of it and slumped back down. "I didn't hit him. I haven't seen him since that night, and Mary has nothing to do with this." Davy's face was contorted with anger. "I called him a no good prick and that's what he was. I didn't hit him. The bastard pinned my arms at my side and butted me with his head. I had a cut and the beginning of a black eye." He pointed to the bridge of his nose. "If Charley hadn't stopped me I'd have knocked his block off." Davy suddenly stopped speaking. Silence permeated the small office.

Davy's voice was softer when he said, "I think he broke my nose. He pushed me down, kicked me. It was Charley that helped me home." Davy rubbed the bridge of his nose, a reminder. "I got a scar. Ask Charley. I didn't hit that bastard."

The chief sat up straight, squared his shoulders and said smoothly and softly, "You were jealous because of Mary. You knew he had been with Mary. What I'm hearing is that he made you look like a fool. He beat you up. Is that why you killed him?"

Before the chief could continue, Davy was on his feet, spilling coffee on his dark wool pants, "Kill him? I didn't kill him. I thought he fell off the wharf. I may have hated him, but I didn't kill him."

"Okay, sit down." With clear authority Crowley had all of Davy's attention. Davy sat heavily in the chair. "Your crewman told me you fired Alonzo after only two weeks fishing with you." The chief paused. "You certainly didn't give him much of a chance. He was fishing on the *Annabella R* after he left your boat. What was the reason you let him go?" Chief Crowley lifted his cup of coffee, but he didn't drink any of it. He watched Davy.

"I told you. Not enough fish, too much crew, we didn't need him. It's another share, you know how it works." Davy was quick to reply.

"Is that after you found out he was seeing Mary Diogo?" The chief saw Davy stiffen. Crowley didn't believe the fisherman was telling him the truth. He pushed a little harder. "You found out about Mary and Alonzo. You fired him. The two of you get into a fight and then Alonzo turns up dead. You know how this looks?"

Davy felt trapped. Wanting this over, he said, "The last time I saw the man was in front of Johnny Mott's bowling alley. I had blood running down my face and I watched the prick turn his back and walk away. Ask Charley." Davy wanted to leave. "I never saw him again." He stood up.

"Sit down Davy, you're not going anywhere. Not just yet." The chief opened his door and called. "Officer Santos." Then he turned to the young fisherman. "Sorry Davy, but I'm going to have to arrest you, for drunk and disorderly. You'll spend the night as our guest. Tomorrow, when you've had a chance to think and sober up we'll talk again."

Davy was too tired to argue. He didn't say a word. He felt hot, like he had a fever. A shiver went through him as he left the room escorted by the officer. He heard the key turn in the lock of the steel cage. Davy lay on the cot, still wearing his coat and boots. The face of Alonzo floated in his mind and he remembered wanting to punch that face when he found out about the two of them. He remembered Alonzo telling jokes. Some pretty funny and others that made Davy blush. Alonzo had a way of talking about women he'd met in the bars on the coast of France, saying they were good at fucking. It made Davy angry without quite knowing why. Now Alonzo was dead. Davy felt as if he were in the water watching his boat move away without him. He pictured Mary's face as he fell asleep.

Down the hall, Crawley was thinking about the conversation he'd had with two of the crewmen on the *Annabella R.* They worked with Alonzo after he stopped fishing with Davy Souza. He sat behind a large desk and leaned back in his chair. The chair came into the office from his home on the day he became chief of police. It rocked, swiveled 380 degrees, had wheels, and had belonged to his father who had taught school.

Taking his notebook from his shirt pocket he reviewed his notes.

Crowley had written about the building that contained Mr. Sklaroff's trucking business, the place where Alonzo had washed up. The chief had checked on top and underneath the pier, to no avail. He reviewed conversations he'd had with different men around the wharfs: fishermen and lumpers, truckers and the bosses in the offices. No one saw anything unusual and no one knew anything about Alonzo. The chief asked about vessels in the harbor toward the end of October, but received vague replies.

But then last evening, Henry Passion, Captain of the *Richard & Arnold* walked into the office. He told the chief that he remembered an unusual ship in the harbor around the end of October. "From Copenhagen the stern said. I saw it with the new binoculars that I got for my birthday." The fisherman talked more about the binoculars than he did about the merchant ship. "I only remembered the ship because a storm drove us in earlier that day. The ship was anchored out a ways from Railroad wharf. I got to try out my new binoculars. I don't remember the name, but I know it said Copenhagen as port of call." When he was leaving the office, Captain Passion told Chief Crowley that it was around October 16 because his birthday was the fifteenth. The chief wasn't sure it would help, but he thanked the captain. The chief looked at his notes. They contained his version of shorthand using symbols and drawings as well as words and abbreviations.

Chief Crowley had spoken to a Boston Detective on three occasions. First time just after the hurricane, about resources and help available if needed. They had met when the Boston officer, by the name of Charles Shiff, came to get Alonzo's body and take it to the medical examiner's office. They talked on the phone when the report was finished. There was nothing new. Alonzo had died of stab wounds and was dead when he entered the water. James Crowley asked Shiff about the ship that brought Alonzo to Provincetown. He wasn't going to give up on finding the vessel. It was a gut feeling that something about it was important. He felt that it was how Alonzo came to town. Maybe it would lead somewhere. In the meanwhile Davy was high on his list of priorities.

Crowley asked the Boston detective if he would check the ship's registry for a match using the information he'd been given. "Even if we find a match, it doesn't mean there is any connection to Alonzo's death," the Boston Police Detective said. Crowley rocked back in his office chair and read again through his notes.

Davy Souza woke with a dry mouth and headache. He felt itchy and worried. At six in the morning he was given breakfast of dry cereal, cold milk, and black coffee. At seven Sergeant Santos unlocked the cell and said, "This way." Their footfalls struck the cement walkway to Chief Crowley's office, not as a parade, not as a death march, and not as a drumbeat. They echoed like a muffled heart beat.

"Sit down Davy." The chief was clean-shaven, and he had on a freshly pressed white shirt under a vest. He opened his notebook. "I wonder if you feel more like talking this morning."

The fisherman wore the same clothing he'd had on for the past four days, rumpled and dirty, smelling of fish and sweat. He looked up. The chief saw sadness in his eyes that quickly turned sharp. Davy squinted and said, "I haven't done anything wrong. I didn't kill him. And if you are going to keep me here then I want a lawyer, I've got rights."

The chief didn't say anything for a few minutes. He got up, came around the desk, and leaned over Davy. "It would be much better for you to tell us the truth now, before we can't help you. You're a town boy and you know we'll help you all we can, but you've got to tell me the truth." The chief waited.

"I told you, I didn't kill him. Maybe you should go ask Jimmy-the-fish-buyer about Alonzo. I hear Alonzo borrowed money from him. Go talk to him, I didn't have anything to do with any of this." The room was hot, small and confining. Then Davy said, "I just want to go fishing, get on my boat and steam away."

Chief Crowley ignored the fisherman and said, "Where were you on December 6?" He waited.

The fisherman jerked his head up, "How the hell should I know, that was over a week ago. Fishing most likely, I'll have to check the logbook." Davy was becoming annoyed with the situation. His voice took on a note of authority. The crew listened when a captain spoke. There was no questioning who was in charge. One boat, one captain, but this time was different. He was not in charge.

There was a light tap on the door. Sergeant Santos came in, stepped around the desk, and said something into the chief's ear. Early that morning, while the fisherman lay sleeping on the hard cot behind bars, Davy's room was searched. A complete set of carving knives was found in the tool shed along with carvings of wooden ducks, seagulls and other small birds. Beautifully done Santos had thought. The officer said that there didn't appear to be any blood on the carving tools, but he brought them along to see if the doc thought there was a match to the wound in Alonzo's chest. Sergeant Santos also whispered to his boss that Davy's cousin said he was with Davy and that the logbook on the boat would confirm the fact that they were out fishing on December 5, 6, and 7.

The chief would talk to the cousin later. He would find out what time the boat came in and where Davy went after that. He said, "Ok Davy, you can get this out and into the open right now. If you've anything to say to me, say it now." Davy looked up into the older man's eyes without saying a word. The only sound was steam coming from the pipes overhead.

Chief Crowley took his time with his reply. "Okay Davy you can go." Crowley straightened his shoulders and went back around the desk. "Just remember, I've got my eyes on you and I will find out if you had anything to do with this." The police chief said out loud. "And right now, it doesn't look good."

Chapter 15

Davy slouched in the wheelhouse chair, hung over, with a morose expression on his face. The temperature was just above freezing and the wind was coming in from the north. The boat moved with a long roll in a swell of four feet, but he didn't seem to notice, just glad to be away from town. He had a headache, was nauseous, and was angry with himself. The first tow that morning had yielded little, a handful of crabs, one lobster and a bushel of flounders. He told Jimmy to climb into the bunk he was going to make this a long tow. The *Fanny Parnell* pulled the net with ease while Davy sat thinking about Alonzo. Helping the guy seemed the right thing at the time, before he'd learned about what was going on with Mary.

When Alonzo first came onboard the *Fanny Parnell* they had joked about Jimmy's fish stew, so full of potatoes you couldn't find a piece of fish in it. Davy remembered laughing with Alonzo. The catch was good at first, but as often happens with fish that have tails, the catch got smaller, less and less in the net. After a third day with little reward Alonzo began chaffing, mumbling under his breath, sipping whiskey when below deck, and grumbling to Jimmy about the catch. "Looks like no pay this week, maybe I should look for job on *Annabella R*. They have hundred boxes." Davy remembered the look on his face when he said, "Why we not go farther to the north?" Davy didn't answer him.

Davy knew very little about the new crewman. The Diogo family had helped him, he was from the Azores, and he knew his way around boats. He did his job. One morning Alonzo had surprised him when he said, "I found a nice little woman." He kissed the ends of his fingers. "*Dolce*, sweet." He had a big smile on his face. Davy was glad for him, Alonzo was happy, fitting into his life in Provincetown. But when the catches became small, two baskets in a tow, Alonzo again challenged the captain. "I see Victor Reis, you know the captain they call *Sheik of Araby*? He and crew they talk about North side of bank, they got hundred boxes, thirty-six hours. Maybe we should go there."

"You can go get a job with the *Shiek* when we get in," Davy replied as he headed to the wheelhouse.

Alonzo was quick, "What? You can't take joke?" The tension eased slightly, but the two men became less friendly as time went by. Alonzo talked of women, the months away from shore, and then landing in big European cities. He bragged about fishing trips that were arduous with weeks and months spent offshore.

Davy pictured Mary Diogo, remembering her as one of the neighborhood girls, five years his junior and a friend. He had been unaware of her beauty until about a year ago when she came into the shop while he was talking to her father. His heart beat faster. Something deep in him awakened. He couldn't take his eyes off her. She had suddenly become a woman. That was a beautiful moment for him, and then came the worst day of his life. On a Sunday morning at St. Peter's Church everything changed for Davy. He saw Mary's face when she looked at Alonzo. It was the smile she had for Alonzo, a knowing smile, sly, excited. Davy felt his heart drop into his stomach. He saw something between them. And then she blushed.

After that morning in church Davy became sullen. He stopped sharing jokes with the crew. He stopped going to his home on Pearl Street, often staying onboard the *Fanny Parnell* docked at the pier. He began drinking at the pool hall and sleeping less. He'd wake and not remember how he got back to the boat. He hated himself for the life he was leading. He felt as if he had lost control and couldn't slow the downward momentum. He wanted everything to go back to the way it was before Alonzo showed up. Mary consumed his thoughts. Davy felt a jealousy that he didn't know existed. What made it worse, embarrassing, was the look Mary gave him. She knew that he knew.

Davy sat in his wheelhouse chair, wanting his thoughts to stop. He felt his stomach twist when he remembered Alonzo's words. They had surprised him but at the time he was glad that Alonzo had found someone. It had been a calm day. He remembered that he could see their breaths against a grey background as they talked. The three men had worked together picking up the last of the five boxes that had spilled on deck. The new crewman had been working on the *Fanny* Parnell for a little over a week when Davy innocently asked, "So Alonzo, what's your life like these days, I mean off the boat? What have you been up to?"

"No *filho da puta,* understand, no pussy these days." Turning his back on the captain he picked up a box and slid it through the hatch to Jimmy who was stacking the catch. Alonzo had said other things about women in the port cities he visited. Davy didn't like dirty talk, but he had laughed all the same. Then came that day in church and Davy began to get a different picture of what Alonzo was up to. When the wash-a-shore immigrant showed up for the next fishing trip Davy was up tight, wanting to holler at the sky. He avoided coming out on deck, instead remaining inside the wheelhouse and letting the two crewmen handle the catch. He fumed all day, smoking one cigarette after another until he was choking.

Again Alonzo began chaffing about the meager catch. Davy came out of the wheelhouse and headed straight for Alonzo. "We're not catching enough fish to keep three men paid. I have to ask you to take your boots with you at the end of this trip. I'll get your pay to you on Friday," the captain said. The other crewman looked at the captain with curiosity, not knowing that there was an ulterior motive to Davy's attitude.

"What? You fire me? I'm best hand you ever got." Alonzo saw the determination on Davy's face. He cleared his throat, sneering, and then spit out, "You piss-ant, you think you better than me. You know nothing." Then words in Portuguese, "*Filho bastardo.*" With that he turned to the foc'sle. At the end of the trip, the lines tied to the poles, Alonzo stepped on deck with boots and oiled jacket in his hand. "You will regret this," he sneered. Davy just shook his head and watched him leave the boat, relieved to see him go.

And now, weeks later, Davy looked at the same surroundings, gray sea, gray sky, thinking about regrets. He pushed thoughts of Alonzo out of his head and wondered why Manny Diogo had acted the way he did the other night on the street. Davy regretted startling him, coming up behind him like that, but Mr. Diogo had spoken to him as if accusing him of something. And he seemed so angry. This added fuel to the injustice Davy was already feeling about how he was treated by Chief Crowley. He decided that he would bring fish to the Diogo's home, as a peace offering, hoping the clouds that hung over them would disappear with the biting North wind.

He could have told Mary the truth. The way Alonzo sometimes spoke about the women he'd met in Portugal and France. He wanted to tell Mary that Alonzo was a chaffer, but Davy didn't say anything because he knew that Alonzo had never mentioned Mary by name. Alonzo never said anything at all about her.

He had tried talking to Mary one afternoon, a few days after Alonzo stopped fishing with him, before he died. Davy followed her home from school. It was spitting snow, enough to cover the ground, filling the air with bright white spots. He had to run to catch up to her at the bottom of the hill on Bradford Street. He asked about her family and school while they walked. She seemed distracted, but when he mentioned

Alonzo, she stopped, turned and looked him in the eyes.

Davy explained, "He's not fishing with me anymore. Got himself a job on a bigger boat." Then Davy said. "Mary, I know it's not my business, but he's not right for you."

Mary's eyes flared. She stared at Davy, incredulous. She started to laugh. "You're jealous." Her look surprised him. She was smiling like she was glad that he was jealous. He began to apologize, but she didn't give him a chance. She picked up her chin, clutched her books tightly to her chest, and walked away into the falling snow. He felt disbelief and disappointment. It was not the unpleasant look that he had expected and this gave him hope. Her eyes had said something else, as if she were glad that Davy was envious. He had noticed her. Davy didn't understand his own feelings much less what was happening between them. Not knowing if he'd made things better or worse had left him completely adrift.

Thinking about Mary he realized now that he hadn't spoken to her since that day. And now the police chief had questioned him about Alonzo. He moved uneasily in his wheelhouse chair, shifting his body, as his eyes searched the surface of the sea, looking at emptiness beyond the small window as if he might find answers there. Was she lost to him? Worrying about Mary, the police, and his future his thoughts seemed to disappear into a fog. Not for the first time, he wished that he'd never carried Alonzo into the Diogo home.

Davy opened the wheelhouse door and yelled, "Jimmy, time to haul back." Always hoping for a full net, this time they were rewarded. The two men filled box after box, working until dark. The town hall clock struck seven when they tied the boat to the pier, knowing their hard work had paid off.

They walked slowly away from the waterfront as soft snow began to fall, disappearing as it touched the ground. His cousin said, "You know Davy if you need to talk, or you want to come by the house sometime, you're always welcome. It's none of my business but I can tell something's eating at you." The town was quiet, stores closed. Jimmy continued, "Crowley asked me a few questions about you. I told him the truth, we were fishing and you'd not harm a fly."

"Yeah, thanks. I'm all right. Sorry, I've been a little tense, but today was good," Davy said. "I'm just worried about money, you understand. The last couple of weeks haven't been so good." Davy reached out to his cousin. They shook hands. "Good-night, Jimmy, I'll see you tomorrow, four o'clock. Get some sleep."

Chapter 16

Davy Souza walked east, to the home where he'd grown up. He had a strange sensation of being watched, but when he stopped and turned, he saw no one. The street was quiet, the snow muffling the noise of his boots. Carrying a string of fish, head down, he trudged home. The porch-light was on when he reached the steps, reflecting Mary as she slipped from the shadows, snow dusting her hat and shoulders, causing her to sparkle in the reflecting glow. As soon as he saw her, a weight was lifted. His weariness melted away, erasing worry, doubt and apprehension.

"Mary, are you alright?" He looked at her carefully. She had lost weight and somehow looked younger.

"I've just come from the Salvador's. I was babysitting. I saw the porch light and I, well, I." She paused, as if unable to finish the sentence.

"Let's go inside. You look cold." Davy couldn't help but smile at her. He realized how much he missed her. He took the fish to the sink, took off his coat and hung it on one of the hooks next to the door. "Would you like something to eat? My mom will have gone to bed, but she always leaves something in the oven." Davy spoke softly not wanting to disturb the quiet of the house.

"Davy I needed to talk to someone. My dad seems to get upset every time I bring up the subject of Alonzo. We had words this evening. He's been so busy with the store and the Fishermen's Ball. It's two weeks away and I guess everyone is excited. They seem to have forgotten all about Alonzo." It came out in a rush, exploding from somewhere within her. "I've already eaten, thanks, you go ahead." They sat at the kitchen table like old friends, as if nothing had changed.

She looked at him. "I'm sorry about everything." Her words hung in the air in the quiet kitchen, taking time for thoughts. She whispered, "I need to tell you something about Alonzo." At the mention of his name Davy bristled. He frowned, keeping his thoughts to himself as Mary continued. "It may be important. He told me about the coins and now that I've had a chance to think about it, I need to explain some things."

Mary looked at Davy. He nodded for her to continue. "I didn't want people to think of him as a thief, but I guess that's what he was." Her lips trembled, but she did not shed a tear. "He took two coins from the pocket of the chief mate before he jumped ship." Mary's loyalty to the dead man was not something Davy wanted to hear about, but he kept silent. She continued. "Alonzo told me that he left the ship in Provincetown Harbor because he didn't like what was happening onboard." Mary stopped and Davy waited. The snow muffled all the outside noise. The kitchen was silent, and then Mary added, "He wanted a new life." Davy grit his teeth.

Her voice grew calm. "Alonzo gave me a gold coin. My parents found it and dad took it to the police chief." Mary explained what the coin looked like and asked if he'd ever seen one. He responded by shaking his head in the negative and looking at her with bewilderment. She added that the police chief didn't think it had anything to do with Alonzo's death. There was silence in the warm kitchen. She hesitated, "But I didn't tell them everything."

Mary looked into Davy's eyes, took a deep breath and continued. "Alonzo said he took two coins from a jacket pocket when he left the ship. It was because he hadn't been paid in six months. The ship was a merchant vessel, a Dutch trawler, the *Zi-der-dik*." She said the name in syllables. "I remember how to say the name, but I'm not sure how to spell it, but that's what it sounded like."

She sighed and continued, "He told me that and more. Do you see? I didn't want him to be remembered as a thief. He wasn't a bad person. And before you say anything, I know you didn't like him, but there's more."

He started to reach across the table to hold her hand, but quickly withdrew. She continued, "Alonzo told me that the boat had stopped in Jamaica to pick up rum, but they also picked up crewmen, crewmen that never left their cabins. He told me that he heard them speaking German." She shivered and tucked her hands into the pockets of her coat.

Davy looked at her with longing. He spoke to her in a gentle voice, "You gave the coin to your father? But you didn't tell them the rest of the story?" There was an affirmative nod. Her faced flushed.

"I guess I should have told the whole story to Chief Crowley when he first asked me about Alonzo, but I was too shocked by his death. At the time I didn't remember anything. And later my father told me he didn't think it had anything to do with Alonzo's death," she added. "He said the coin was worth a lot of money. It's solid gold. Chief Crowley kept it and I didn't think any more about it. My father told me that I would get the coin back." There was a scowl on her face. "I didn't want everyone to think of Alonzo as a bad person, he wasn't." The sentence reverberated, echoing inside the small kitchen. When Davy didn't say anything she continued, "The Chief said that Alonzo's death was an accident. Now I'm not sure I believe him. Mom and dad seem so worried all the time. They hover over me like hawks."

What she told Davy next took him completely by surprise. "Alonzo said that this trawler was bringing people into the country. He said there was a plan to meet a fishing boat offshore and bring the people to Boston. But because of the storm they had to seek shelter in Provincetown harbor. It was the closest port. That's how he came to be here."

Davy interrupted her. "This could be important, Mary. You did the right thing telling me." He remembered how angry her father seemed to be the other night. Maybe they could talk again in the morning. This time maybe he'd listen to what Davy had to say. Davy didn't think the death of Alonzo was an accident. Not after how he'd been questioned by Chief Crowley.

Davy decided to tell Mary about what had happened to him. "Chief Crowley had me in for a talk the other night. He said some things that made it sound like the police think I may have had something to do with Alonzo's death." Davy paused, watching the snow as it melted into her black hair, glistening, and then disappearing. He broke the silence and surprised Mary by saying, "I had a fight with Alonzo." He stopped, nodded his head a few times, and then continued, "Don't look at me like that. I didn't start it, but we did get into it, and now Crowley thinks I had something to do with his death."

He reached his hand out to her and then withdrew it. "What you've told me about men speaking German and the stolen gold coins could be important. Tell your parents when you get home, tonight." Davy had been reading the newspapers and understood that Germany was building an army. They had a new military, a new form of government and a new leader. There were rumors of work camps, forced labor, and innuendos that the leader was ruling with an iron fist. Davy heard on the radio comments about a totalitarian government, a form of hero worship gone amiss, so that world leaders were beginning to look at the German regime in a new light. Oppression and violence was spreading. Words of war were spoken.

Davy Souza had more urgent worries. He said, "Maybe the police can trace the boat. It may help." Even with the oven warming the kitchen, Davy felt a chill, "Mary you said two coins. What happened to the other?"

"I don't know and I don't care. I also don't care what the coins may be worth." They looked at each other. "However much, it's not worth killing for." A hint of anger flashed in her eyes, but this was not the time to speak of their own feelings. She said, "I don't want to talk about Alonzo anymore. Okay?"

He nodded while thinking that this could lead to another set of problems. The man who owned the coins would want them back. They were valuable. Perhaps the murderer was after the coins. That could involve Mary. Maybe there were more coins or more to the story. Davy said, "Tell your dad everything: about the boat, the coins and the men." He didn't voice his opinion that there may be more coins out there and someone was looking for them. Davy suddenly realized that he needed to keep a close eye on Mary. He added, "Chief Crowley will want to know."

She looked at his dark brown eyes and said, "I know you couldn't have had anything to do with his death." Her smile could melt his heart. She repeated, "It couldn't have anything to do with you. I've known you all my life. You would never kill anything, except fish of course." They shared a small laugh.

The tension eased. Davy said, "I do appreciate the vote of confidence, but there have been times when I wished Alonzo had never been born." Davy could see this upset and surprised her. There was vehemence in his words, "I'm not sorry he's gone, but believe me; I didn't have anything to do with killing him."

He took her hand, briefly, feeling the softness of her skin against his callused palms. She picked up her head, looking him in the eyes as if seeing him for the first time. "I believe you." She stood up. "I'll talk to my dad, tonight." Davy opened the door for her and she turned and kissed him on the cheek. "Thanks for listening. I've got to go."

"Wait." Davy was pulling on his jacket. "I'll walk you home." He wanted to protect her, stay close to her for as long as possible, and he had a nagging feeling that trouble was on the wind. He would never let anything bad happen to her, not if he could help it, not while he was alive.

He lay awake that night, seeing her face and trying to recall the feeling of her lips on his cheek. He was smiling when he fell asleep. He dreamt of coins falling from the sky while Mary stood on a dune calling to him. Alonzo was grinning at him, holding a knife above his head ready to bring it down on his chest. Davy sucked in cold morning air as he awoke. It was dark outside and he shivered. He could see his breath. As he gathered his long underwear and wool socks his first thoughts were, *"Mary could be in danger."* The dream hung in the air like a mist shrouding some buried truth.

Davy didn't go fishing that day. He greeted his mother, ate quickly and swallowed a cup of coffee before going out into a quiet grey morning. He hurried to the *Fanny Parnell* to tell his crewman that they weren't going out today. Jimmy could work on deck, mend some holes in the net or clean up the foc'sle. The boat would stay at the dock. He planned to follow Mary until she was safely in school and then head to the chandlery to speak to Manny Diogo. Davy knew the police were looking to him as a suspect, while Mary, somehow, was unintentionally involved in a murder, and possibly at risk. Davy's problem began and ended with her. She never turned around as he watched her walk to school with her sisters.

Later that morning the owner of the *Fanny Parnell* entered the chandlery and looked around. Manny wasn't anywhere in sight. Davy thought how trusting Manny was to leave the shop unlocked and unattended. As he had done many times before, he went through the open door into the hall that led to the kitchen. As he stepped across the threshold into the dark hall he heard words echoing. Manny was shouting. Davy stopped in his tracks and held his breath.

Manny's voice rose, harsh and angry, "Keep her away from Davy. I don't care what she said. This is different." He heard the slap of his hand on the table. Manny was hollering at his wife. It felt so wrong to hear him yelling like that. "He could be dangerous. We can't allow Mary to spend time with him." Manny's voice echoed into the hallway. And then it became very quiet.

Davy felt stupid, trapped. He heard Manny continue, but not in such a loud and furious way, "Don't look at me like that Eleanor. You didn't hear it the way Chief Crowley put it. This is murder we are talking about." There was a scrape of a chair, and then Manny said, "Keep Mary home after school and away from Davy Souza." Davy didn't hear the last sentence. He had already left the shop. His black eyebrows knit together, scowling. With his hands jammed down into his coat pockets he walked toward the center of town, in the direction of the wharf where he kept his *Fanny Parnell* docked. He wished he'd gone fishing that morning.

In the kitchen behind Manny's Ship Chandler, all was quiet. It was settled. Eleanor said, "Beware of absolute certainty." She picked up the dishes and went to the sink. Looking out her kitchen window she said, "I used to love this view, Manny, now it just looks cold." She turned to her husband, "I believe Mary. Davy Souza wouldn't hurt a fly."

Chapter 17

A large ice flow was spotted in Wellfleet, off Billingsgate Shoal. Word spread among the fishermen, keeping the boats tied up. A shift in wind direction could bring the ice to Provincetown, locking out any boat that was not already inside the harbor. Davy kept the *Fanny Parnell* tied to the wharf where he usually unloaded his catch. He checked her lines and bilges two times a day while he waited for a change in the weather. For the next few days he followed Mary to and from school, staying well behind and out of sight. She remained at home during the late afternoon and evening.

The loneliness that sometimes comes with the depths of winter descended upon the town, the harbor and the Diogo house, bringing feelings of isolation.

Manny Diogo was worried, but did not share his concerns with his family. He was sometimes sharp with his daughters, unusual for him. A fragile peace settled over the household after Eleanor told her husband that everyone felt like they were walking on eggshells around him. He spent time in the shop and went to the Legion Hall. Eleanor went to the attic to paint when the girls were at school. The family seemed to returning to something like a normal routine. Mary carried herself more erect, laughing with her sisters and sometimes singing softly with the RKO station. Life would go on.

And then on Friday, January 16, 1939, Chief James Crowley was called in the early morning hours to the cold-storage building on Sklaroff Wharf. It was exactly one month since the body of Alonzo was discovered. He climbed the stairs to the second floor, feeling as if he carried the weight of the town on his shoulders. His heavy footfalls sounded on each of the wooden steps like large books being slammed shut. He made his way to the office of Jimmy-the-fish-buyer. The walled off space was in the back on the second floor. A fisherman had called asking the operator to send the police. He had found Jimmy-the-fish-buyer. "He is lying on the floor of his office. He's dead," the man said.

Charles Forrest owned and ran the *Angeline*. He was sitting on a chair outside the closed door with his head in his hands, elbows on his knees. Officer Lewis was standing next to him. He opened the door when he saw the chief and pointed into the office at the body. The two men stepped across the threshold. Lewis explained in a nervous and hurried voice. "It's bad. I told Captain Forrest to wait outside and gave him a chair. He's pretty shook up."

Blood was pooled on the floor, under, and around the old man. Chief Crowley's hands shook as he examined the body. He felt for a pulse at the side of his neck, but could not detect one. He bent his head, placing his ear to the man's mouth, listening for any sound of life. He detected none. Jimmy's skin was grey. The chief had seen the man at the Selectmen's meeting a couple of days ago. The warmth of his life had seeped into the wooden floor of the office. "Damn it. What the hell is going on?" The chief stood up.

His Sergeant said, "Mr. Forrest told me that Jimmy kept cash in here, sometimes a lot of money. Could be a robbery gone wrong. The safe is open."

The chief nodded then said, "Help me roll him over onto his back." The fish buyer was wearing a shirt and sweater, both soaked in blood, beginning to congeal. He wore suspenders attached to his woolen pants. Everything was now covered in a sticky, dark mess. There was a smell of metal, like iodine, rusting iron, and seawater. The chef said, "I'll speak to Captain Forrest. Then I want you to take him to the office, get a statement on paper. Take the patrol car and bring back a camera and the new fingerprint kit from my office. I'll call Doc Rice and Mr. Richland." His mind was building thoughts as fast as he could produce them.

The patrolman nodded. "Yes sir," he said.

The chief continued, "I don't want anything touched in here." The chief walked to the desk and looked around. The safe with its door wide open was situated behind the desk. Papers from the desk had spilled onto the floor. The desk drawers were open, rifled, the middle one turned upside down onto the floor. A wooden filing cabinet sat in the corner, the drawers closed. James Crowley bent over the safe. "I'll see his wife when I'm done here," the chief said. "I want to know who helps Jimmy with the bills, his bookkeeper. I want to know what's missing from this safe, the desk and this whole place." Then the chief swore again under his breath.

Crowley stepped out of the office into a large open area surrounded by cement walls. Large wooden doors hung from rollers on a track at one end. Crowley looked at stacks of wooden boxes, kegs of nails, and piles of nets that lay on the floor of the large room as if waiting for better days. The chief was thinking, *Someone could hide in there if he wanted.* The fisherman, holding his wool cap, looked up. The chief said, "Sorry about this Mr. Forest, but I need to ask you a couple of questions. Are you okay?" When the fishing captain nodded, the chief continued, "Can you tell me what brought you here and how you found him?"

The police chief watched the fisherman's jaw tighten as he clenched his teeth. He looked pale, like he might throw up. He said, "I came to pick up some money that Jimmy owed me. I took fish out with him last week. I saw him on the street yesterday and he said to stop in the office this morning." The fisherman took a moment to brush his hands across his face, rubbing his eyes with the tips of his long fingers. "Jimmy told me he'd be here by five. I got here around five-thirty." He took deep breaths. He put his cap on, and then took it off again, combing his hand through his dark hair.

Crowley asked, "Did you see anyone when you came up the wharf?" Captain Forrest shook his head. The police chief continued, "Was anyone near the building when you got here?" The police chief put his hand on the man's shoulder. The fisherman shook his head, no.

"Why would anyone do this?" Charles Forrest said. He looked at the chief. "Everyone knows Jimmy, likes him. I mean this makes no sense." He hesitated, again running his hand through his hair. "He's been in Provincetown his whole life." Jimmy had fished for over twenty years before starting his own trucking business. The fisherman added, "He's on the advertising committee for the ball, for Christ sake." As if that would explain why he should still be alive.

The policeman put his hand on the fisherman's shoulder and continued his questioning, "I know this has been a shock, but think back. Did you notice anything unusual when you arrived?"

The fisherman shook his head, "No. It's cold and I had my collar up and my head down. I wasn't looking around, just where I was walking. The planks on the wharf are uneven and it was still dark."

"Do you remember seeing any boats tied to the unloading door?" The chief motioned toward the large sliding doors. Again the fisherman shook his head.

Captain Forrest said, "I think I remember hearing an engine when I got to the office."

The chief asked, "A boat engine?"

"No, a car or maybe a small truck. I remember thinking at this hour it might be a fish truck leaving for the city, but for some reason it sounded more like a car, a gas job, smooth, not like the diesel trucks that Jimmy uses to ship his fish."

Crowley said, "Thanks for your help Charles. Sergeant Lewis will take you to the station and then home. Please write down everything you just told me and anything else that you remember. Wait here while I have a word with Lewis." The policeman's voice was quiet, the words soft. He left the man to his own thoughts and walked back into the crime scene.

Inside the office with the door closed, the chief spoke quietly to the Sergeant, "Call Patrolman Santos when you get to the station. He's most likely home sleeping. It's his day off, but we need him. Don't give out any information over the phone. You know Mildred will listen in. If he puts up a fuss, tell him the chief wants him to stay at the station this morning, overtime pay. After you have Santos at the desk, get Captain Forest home, and then come back here. I'll wait for the doc and the hearse." He knew the town would be crazy with rumors soon enough. "When I'm done here I'd like you to stay around the office and talk to anyone that comes around the ice house today, fishermen, lumpers, truck drivers, anyone that shows up."

After Lewis and Captain Forest left the chief looked around the large open space. It was a hundred feet to the back of the building. There were closed doors on two sides, but both big hanging doors were shut. The chief walked across the damp floor and pulled on the handle of the sliding door on his right. He was surprised by how easily the sixteen-foot door moved on the track. The chief looked at the cold water of Provincetown Harbor directly below him. He leaned his head out and looked around at the building. It stood on pillars of wood surrounded on three sides by black rippling saltwater. The water of the bay was six feet below and he was very near to where Alonzo had been found. Daylight was sweeping across the eastern horizon, nautical twilight. He could see the shadows of fishing boats anchored to the west, other piers in the distance, but there was no boat tied below or at the front of this cold storage building.

Crowley paced ten feet, stopped, and returned to the office. He spoke to himself as he wrote in his notebook. "I need to find out if Jimmy had any enemies? Who are the regular fishermen who come here? What boats unload here? Find out about his business dealings." The police chief was writing furiously. He added: where was Davy Souza? Crowley's mind was racing.

Fifteen minutes later Doc Rice entered the room followed by Mr. Richland and a man that worked for the undertaker. Doctor Rice pronounced Jimmy deceased. The body was wrapped tightly in blankets and carried down the stairs by the four men. Half an hour later Chief Crowley sat with Jimmy's wife. He was gentle and she was helpful. She sat in a soft overstuffed chair and held rosary beads in her hands, working them continuously. She spoke with a heavy Portuguese accent. She said that Jimmy had left for the office around four-thirty. "He has trouble sleeping. His rheumatism bothers him and he likes to be early on the wharf. He likes to see the sun rise," she said. Her face was pale. Tears flowed down her cheeks, but she remained calm. She told him that Jimmy didn't have a secretary, "He wrote everything down and kept neat files on what came in and what went out. He kept money in the safe, but usually not much. "It varies with how much fish is coming in coming out of the boats." She bowed her head, murmuring, fingering the small beads.

The chief asked about the safe. She said it was kept locked when he wasn't there. Crowley unbuttoned his coat, talked to the widow about Jimmy, and waited with her until a sister came to stay with her. Before he left he said, "I'm sorry for your loss and if there is anything I can do, just call. " She hugged him when he bent to say goodbye. Jimmy's death had brought them closer, forever bonding them in tragedy.

Chapter 18

It didn't take long for word to spread through the coastal village. The old man known as Jimmy-the-fish-buyer had been found dead in his office. Some folks didn't believe the rumors of blood and gore, but that didn't change the facts. A few felt that evil had come to their community and they went to church to pray. Crowley knew about this kind of evil. It could be caught and brought to justice. He would do everything in his power to seek it out and remove whoever was responsible.

"We will get to the root of these murders," the chief said. He told his two patrolmen the details of the crime then added, "We need to keep a lid on the rumor mill. And there are some things only we will know. There will be no talk about the details, the wounds, the time of death, or what his office looked like. Am I clear." The officers understood that their chief meant business. Their heads bobbed in agreement.

Whispers around town of murder remained veiled in innuendo and gossip. Jimmy died between four and five o'clock in the morning, less then an hour before the body was found. It was confirmed by Dr. Rice that the two men, Alonzo and Jimmy, had met their deaths in the same way, cessation of life from stab wounds. A similar weapon was used for both.

The chief and his sergeant examined the papers in the file cabinet, in the safe, and on the desk. Jimmy was not in debt and had not received any large unaccounted for payments. The chief felt sure that something had been taken from the safe. Crowley said, "We're dealing with cold blooded murder." He had slept badly during the previous month, and now this. He wondered if he'd ever sleep through the night again. His mind whirled. "It could be that the murderer let himself in before Jimmy arrived and was waiting for him in the dark. I'll bet Jimmy didn't lock that door at the top of the stairs. I think someone was looking for something."

Officer Lewis added his thought, "Or maybe Jimmy knew the murderer, met him at the door and let him in." This meant the murderer had walked up the outside stairs, in the front door, a calculated risk.

The chief spoke, "It would be taking a chance. The wharfs come awake early. There was no moon last night and the cold keeps the waterfront quiet. Maybe we'll get lucky. Someone may have seen something." On this January morning it was quiet around the waterfront. The ice flow that locked in Wellfleet harbor was keeping the fishing boats of Provincetown close to home. No boats had left their berths.

Even as a child Officer Lewis liked watching the boats, keeping track of their coming and goings. "Our fishermen are a tight knit group. Someone would have noticed a boat moving around." The fishermen that he'd spoken to stated that boat traffic had come to a standstill.

Chief Crowley replied, "The murderer had to have balls to do this. Walking away without being seen. Using the stairway was risky. He could have run into someone like Captain Forrest coming in to see Jimmy. I'm thinking that Jimmy caught someone in the act of stealing."

The two policemen were in the fish buyer's office. The chief sat in the desk chair looking at a ledger with lists of names, dates, amounts of fish unloaded and amounts of money paid out. Officer Lewis was on his knees, placing items in a box and making a list of what the safe contained.

The chief rose from the desk and said, "This is interesting. Seems Jimmy gave Alonzo money and it was not paid back. I'm going back to the office. I need to make a phone call." He looked at his coworker, "Stay here. Please make a record of what is in the safe, and anything in the desk drawers. List everything you think may be important. I'm taking this ledger to the station with me." The only thing of interest was the account showing Alonzo's name.

Chief Crowley was at the police station fifteen minutes later, his notebook open and the phone in his left hand when Manny Diogo walked in and sat down. The shopkeeper was eager to share some news of his own. "I thought I should tell you what my daughter said last night." Manny watched the chief return the phone to its cradle. "She told me that Alonzo had two coins when he arrived in town. One he gave to her. But as to where the other one went, she doesn't know." It had only been five hours since Jimmy's body was found and the chief was sure that Manny Diogo had not heard about it.

The chief was biting the end of his mustache, debating how much to say to his friend. "Jimmy-the-fish-buyer would have been just the man to see if someone was looking for cash." It was not a question and Crowley didn't wait for a reply. He said, "Maybe the coin was given as collateral for a loan." The chief looked exhausted but his friend looked confused. Crowley told Manny what had happened that morning.

Manny was shocked, "You think the murders are connected and have something to do with the coins?" He looked at the chief and repeated, "Would someone actually commit murder for a gold coin?"

The police chief shook his head. "Unlikely that it was the only reason, but then again, maybe the murderer was caught in the act of stealing and was recognized?" Crowley added, "At this point it could be anything. Just the same I'm going to have another talk with Davy Souza. I'll be making a call to Boston as well."

Manny's eyebrows were almost touching. He looked at the floor then up to scowl at his friend. "Surely you don't think Davy could have anything to do with this. I have to wonder why Davy would steal a coin, even if he knew about it. Mary told me that Davy didn't know anything about the gold coins. They spoke last night." The shopkeeper told the policeman everything his daughter had said about Alonzo, the coins and the ship.

Manny added, "Davy's never been in trouble. He makes a decent living fishing. And besides, Davy's known Jimmy all his life and this is cold-blooded murder you're talking about. I can't picture Davy like that." Manny had listened to Mary and to Eleanor, both were sure of the fishermen's innocence.

The chief was not convinced, "That's why he's not sitting in a cell right now. That and I don't have any proof that Davy is involved," The police chief made a growling noise. There was anger in both men's eyes. The chief broke the silence, "Don't worry, we'll get whoever did this."

After Manny had closed the door behind him, James opened his notebook, writing names, dates and questions. The phone rang. The chief recognized the voice on the other end as Charles W. Shiff, from the

State Police Office. During the past three months the two men had spoken over the phone on a number of occasions, just after the hurricane about relief efforts, and then later when Alonzo's body was found. The state police had taken Alonzo's body to the county morgue in Pocasset. They spoke minimum pleasantries. The man from Boston went straight to his reason for calling. "Chief, I'd like to talk to you about your murdered man."

"Which one? I was just about to call you. We have another victim, stabbing, same as the first." The chief gave Detective Shiff the details of the latest crime. "I was just about to call you."

Shiff said he had something else in mind. "You can fill in the details of the second victim when I see you. I'll arrange for transport of the body to the state medical examiner." Shiff was breathing heavily into the phone. He continued, "I'm coming to Provincetown tomorrow and I'll be bringing someone with me. We'd like to sit down face to face. We'll be in your office first thing tomorrow morning, around nine o'clock." Crowley was told he would be meeting a representative of a newly formed branch of the United States Government. The chief was impressed by the words Federal Bureau of Investigation.

Chapter 19

While Chief Crowley sat at his desk wondering why the FBI was interested in this small fishing village, Manny Diogo headed across Commercial Street to the second floor and the Legion Hall where men had gathered to attend the last meeting before the Fishermen's Ball. The room was crowded. Cigarette smoke filled the air and a buzz of excitement could be heard in the voices. There was a sudden burst of laughter and Manny watched Carlos slap Big Billy on the back, friends sharing a joke.

Manny had been carrying around feelings of suspicion, anger and danger. He had acknowledged these feelings to his wife the previous night, telling her that he didn't like the way rumors were spreading. She said this horrible tragedy brought out the worst in people, but with time it would blow over. She told her husband that he had no control over what others said. "Be patient," Eleanor said, "Things will be back to normal in no time."

His thoughts were pulled away from his wife and back into the room when Captain John Russe stepped up to the front and began banging a gavel on the table. Manny wondered where he'd found something that belonged in the judge's chamber across the street. "Everyone, may I have your attention." The room settled. "Thank you for the work you've done. We have raised $3,580.00 so far. You can all be proud when we hand the check to Mrs. William Bangs of the American Red Cross." He took a breath and continued, "And because of your efforts the Provincetown Ladies Aid will also share in the profits. We have much to celebrate." A cheer went up and clapping sounded around the hall. Someone whistled and the room again grew quiet. "Before I continue about the ball, I'd like to ask for a moment of silence for our colleague and friend, James Souza, better known as Jimmy-the-fish-buyer. As some of you know may know, he died this morning. That's all I know." He stopped speaking while the room settled. "He was a good man and we'll all miss the old coot." A silence fell over the room as if someone had hit a switch. Each man was left with his own thoughts. Some lowered their heads while others looked around the room, questioning, curious, unaware of the fish buyer's demise. Manny met the eyes of Davy Souza before the room returned to life. Davy had a look of surprise on his face.

After a long pause Captain Russe added without his usual buoyancy, "We are hoping to make this Fishermen's Ball an annual event, an anniversary ball. It will be a signal for the gathering of all fishermen, their families, and friends in the spirit of festivity and good fellowship." He took a deep breath and bellowed,

197

"Thank you for making this affair possible." The clapping that followed was light and petered out within seconds, as if the shadow of Jimmy's demise had passed over the room. And then Russe raised a hand and bellowed, "One more thing. In back, near the door, are the booklets for the ball. Everyone should take one home. We will be giving them out to folks at the door. This meeting is adjourned."

Men began moving. This gathering was slow to break up, some needing to hear more, and everyone wanting a copy of the booklet. Some men had questions about Jimmy-the-fish-buyer. They huddled together shaking their heads in disbelief. A steady murmur of voices could be heard around the room as the news of Jimmy's death circulated. In this close knit community rumors surrounding a death caused jaws to clench. Uncertainty, fear, and sadness were passed from man to man. Each person in the room would deal with death in their own way. Most of the men left the room quietly. They would show the booklet to their families and pass along the terrible news about Jimmy-the-fish-buyer.

Davy stayed behind to help clear the tables and chairs. The noise in the hall diminished as coats were pulled on and the door opened and closed. Manny walked to where he had left his coat on the back of his chair. Frank Rosa was doing the same. Frank buttoned his coat against the cold January night. "Terrible news about Jimmy, he was a good old man, always helping others. This is just terrible." The barber waited for a second then said, "I guess I'll see you at the dance."

Manny sat down in one of the folding chairs thinking about what he'd been told by Chief Crowley. Manny's stomach was upset. He wanted to get home. He sighed, stood, and was buttoning his overcoat when Davy Souza approached him. "Mr. Diogo, I hope you can believe me when I tell you I had nothing to do with Alonzo's death." He looked the older man right in the eyes as he spoke, his face serious. The young captain slowly shifted his stance from side to side, legs slightly apart, swaying as if he were standing on the deck of his *Fanny Parnell*.

Manny had always liked the kid. He put his hand on the fisherman's shoulder and said, "Davy, there seems to be more to all this than we realized. Maybe we can work together to see if we can make sense of what is happening here in our town." He paused, "What do you say?" Manny put out his hand. Davy took it and smiled. The shopkeeper's hands were smooth, less calloused than the fisherman's, but they both contained character. They shook hands without pressure, strong, and lasting. They might one day be friends. The age difference, the emotions under the surface, and the feelings that neither would speak of, gave their relationship distance and propriety.

They sat at the table in the empty hall and talked for another half hour without coming to any conclusions. They didn't know anyone who would have reason to kill the two men. They agreed to share any information that might have bearing on either murder. They discussed the second coin. Who would want it? Could there be more? The shopkeeper said, "I've already spoken to Chief Crowley about the boat and the people on board."

Davy added, "He questioned me about Alonzo, kept me overnight, but he didn't tell me anything, just asked a lot of questions."

"I heard all about that. He didn't have any proof against you and had to let you go. But what Mary told me last night went straight to Chief Crowley this morning. I believe that this news might be important." Manny hesitated before adding, "There's always the possibility that the two deaths aren't related. But my thinking is that they must be. I've lived here all my life and I've never seen anything like this. Of course the chief doesn't tell me everything, so I'm just assuming they were killed by the same person." They were the only men left in the room, alone with their own thoughts.

Davy said, "I'll do whatever I can to help you."

Manny's dark brooding feelings began lifting. He believed Davy. Manny had never felt quite right when it came to Alonzo. He was worldly. Their small fishing village didn't match up to big cities where Alonzo had spent his earlier years. He had to be cunning, sly and maybe even a shade dangerous in order to survive in the coastal cities of Europe. Manny felt sure that the dead seamen had seen the seedier side of life. He remembered feeling sorry for the boy when he had stayed in their home, but at the same time he had not trusted him. The shopkeeper thought about the police chief's reasons for believing that Davy might have reason for wanting Alonzo dead. He was well aware of the feelings that Davy had for his daughter. But killing with a knife, up close and personal, was another story. Davy might be a bit of a loner because of his line of work, but Manny trusted him.

Jimmy the-fish-buyer was a friend to hard working fishermen and Manny couldn't see a motive for Davy killing him. He didn't believe Davy to be a thief, even if he knew about the coins. And Mary had said that Davy didn't, so how could he believe that Davy was capable of murder. Alonzo, on the other hand, was a different story. He was like a fish out of water. What did they really know about his life before the man arrived in Provincetown? Manny hadn't known him very long, but he trusted his own feelings. He said to Davy, "Cone on, we can talk as we walk. I'd like to get home." The pair headed for the door and down the wooden steps.

The streets were quiet. Stores and businesses along Commercial Street were closed and dark. The air was damp, crisp, and brittle as if snow would begin at any moment. The streetlights glowed, reflecting the image of the two men walking side by side. The shopkeeper was taller by six inches. They were different ages, but they wanted the same things. Davy broke the silence. "When friends share, help each other, they can accomplish good things like the dance. But this murder business is vile. I've never thought I'd see anything like this and I don't like it." They finished the walk without speaking. The only noise came from the Town Hall clock chiming nine strikes. It was three days before the Fishermen's Association's First Anniversary Ball.

Chapter 20

The dance was held at eight o'clock on Thursday night. It was traditional for fishermen to take Friday off, keeping the boat tied to the dock or on the mooring. The captains used the time to pay the crew and to work on the boats. The nets would be hauled up and mended. The gear was greased, chains inspected, engine cleaned, all in constant need of tending. As any fishermen will tell you, "Rust never sleeps." The salt disintegrates iron over time. It wears the woolens and the winter wind wears the lines. Having the ball on a Thursday gave the workingmen time to recover, the unspoken tradition. The crewmen took the day off to bring their pay home to families. Fish buyers caught up on what had been unloaded the previous week. The dance was a bonus, a reward for their hard work, long hours and little pay. On the Friday after the dance most of the fishermen had the day off.

The women were having fun with the excitement. Most didn't care what day the dance was held. It was an opportunity to be out of the house, listening to real live music, watching the sparkle of the other ladies. For weeks the females in the Diogo household had been dancing around the parlor with the radio playing louder than usual. The girls sang along with the swinging songs of Glenn Miller. A favorite on the radio was Ray Noble and his orchestra playing *Way Down Yonder in New Orleans* with Miller on the trombone, Charlie Spivak and Pee Wee Erwin on trumpets. Manny in his shop could feel the thumping sounds from above and it made him smile. Things were retuning to normal.

On the evening of the big dance Mary and her mother spent time together in front of the mirror. Eleanor was dressed in a floor-length gown of taffeta. She wore a string of pearls around her neck with earrings to match. They had been a gift from her parents on her wedding day. Looking in the mirror at her daughter she said, "You are turning into a lovely woman, Mary. You look beautiful." Their eyes met.

"There is much love in the world." Eleanor said, "And I know you will find it again." Mary's smile was the reassurance that her mother needed. Mary's dress came to mid-calf, was dark blue, made of soft crape. She wore a sweater of a matching dark blue. Her hair was pulled up in front and fixed with two combs. She looked beautiful.

Half an hour later mother and daughter walked into the living room and were greeted by Manny along with their neighbor, Mrs. Rogers, who would keep the two younger sisters company. Eleanor and Mary wrapped their new dresses in their old woolen coats. Compliments and laughter followed the adults as they left their home and headed for the center of town.

The sounds of music and laughter could be heard from a block away coming in waves when the doors to the Town Hall opened. People were arriving, greeting each other in the lobby before ascending the two wide staircases that flanked either side of the entrance. Even with the temperature at freezing the town's citizens had come out in force.

The three Diogos hurried into an auditorium where people were waving to one another, laughing at nothing. They headed for the stairs. The large auditorium had been transformed by dimming lights, hanging paper lanterns, and the irresistible sounds of an orchestra playing *Music, Maestro, Please,* that bouncy tune Tommy Dorsey gave to the world. The Boston Orchestra was pounding out a good rendition and people were getting into the swing. Small groups from the teenage set were doing a rendition of the *jitterbug* as the adults looked on in amazement. This gathering of people in fancy dress was a first for many in the room. With the sounds of music came the tapping of feet, it was impossible to keep still. Everyone wanted to dance.

While their parents, families, neighbors and friends tapped their feet to the rhythm, the youngsters bounced and bobbed, dipped and swayed, moving their bodies in a new form of dance. The room was quickly filling and the mood was zestful, animated and playful. "Save a dance for me Mary," her father said. She gave him the gift of a wide smile, a kiss his cheek, and then left to find her friends who were nearer to the stage. Manny and Eleanor headed to the tables set up along the back wall where a few committee members had gathered for a cup of beer costing ten cents. Whiskey was available for a quarter. Frank Rosa and his wife were standing at the table when Manny and Eleanor arrived.

They shook hands. Frank leaned in and said to Manny, "I understand that Carlos donated a couple kegs of beer, a case each of rum and whiskey. He's bringing in more trucking business, doing well I hear."

"Good for him. I haven't seen him in over a week." Manny said. His words had no enthusiasm. He had no wish to ruin Eleanor's evening with talk about Carlos or any talk of rumors, but Manny was curious. "Is Carlos here tonight? I don't see him."

Frank Rosa raised his shoulders and shook his head. "I haven't seen him."

Manny looked around the large auditorium, happy to see so many faces he recognized. Everyone was either standing watching the band or moving around the floor with a bouncy beat. The dancing had begun.

Manny spotted Davy Souza standing on the opposite side of the hall leaning against the wall. Manny wanted to ask him if he'd heard anything around the wharf, anything that might help. He leaned into his wife and spoke loud enough to be heard over the sounds. "Eleanor, I'd like to say hello to Davy. I'll be back in a minute."

The music swelled. Eleanor's eyes caught his and her head bobbed in tempo, up and down, in the affirmative. Manny stopped and shook hands with Sivert Benson and his wife. The woman was bouncing and grinning, no doubt waiting for her husband to ask her to dance. Then Big-Billy Segura approached him and shouted about the great turnout they had. By the time Manny reached the spot where he'd seen Davy the crowd had grown thick, concealing any trace of the fisherman. He was gone.

Manny returned to his wife. He knew she wanted to dance, so he took her by the hand, and moved closer to the dance floor. They joined the others who stood at edge of the huge auditorium to watch the teenagers do the latest version of the new dance steps. Eleanor hollered to Manny, "We can wait for a slower song and do a foxtrot around the room." Manny nodded in agreement.

Manny had not seen Davy move closer to the front of the ballroom. Davy had his eyes on Mary. A group of classmates surrounded her, making it difficult for Davy to keep her in sight. He moved in her direction. The room seemed to be growing with people, sounds and motion. The high school girls reminded him of his own school days. He'd spent more time fishing than in the classroom, but managed to graduate. Davy believed the knowledge that came from many places and that experience is reward in itself. He was his own boss and proud of it. Davy was a reader and enjoyed listening to the radio. His world was small, but he had a philosophical perspective on life from watching the turn of the tides, the dawning of each new day, and from watching the stars rotated in the heavens. Poetic thoughts stirred him. At the same time he felt a stir of jealousy, a feeling that he was becoming more familiar with. He watched Mary and her friends. "So close and yet so far away," he said out loud. No one heard him above the music, talk, and laughter.

Davy watched Mary moving her head from side to side in time with the music when her friend Susan Jahnig came up to her, leaned in covering her mouth with her hand, telling her something. The words brought Mary's head up straight. She fluttered her hands up and down, smiled, and looked toward the opposite side of the room. Her face showed surprised and she nodded her head at her friend. Davy watched as she moved toward the other end of the stage. She was moving quickly.

He lost track of her for a moment. People were spinning and jumping, others dancing a foxtrot. There was movement all around the hall. The music became more jubilant and then the big room went from jitterbug to the *Beer Barrel Polka*. Hundreds of people did their best to shake the house. The excitement grew. There was shouting, laughter and hooting. It felt like a wild frenzy, a cry of freedom or the last hurrah. The town-folk had let their hair down. Fishermen and insurance men, car dealers and truck drivers, mechanics and bankers moved to the Polish beat in a circle around the room.

Davy was getting closer to the front of the auditorium, heading in the direction that Mary had gone. He turned when he heard his name called, "Davy." He was looking at Manny Diogo who had seen the fisherman once again. Manny caught up with Davy and called to him, but instead of answering, Davy turned without speaking and headed toward the stage leaving Manny standing there, bewildered, astonished and angry. Davy Souza bolted from the side door of the hall following after Mary.

At the same time, on the other side of the music filled auditorium, Chief Crowley pushed open the massive wooden doors that led to the stairs and then the street. He felt the night air sting his face as he caught sight of Davy Souza running across Commercial Street toward the waterfront. Crowley paused. There was a moment of confusion as he wondered where Davy was going. Romance was alive inside the town hall, but Crowley took no notice of the great building's glowing lights or the moody tune echoing from within. He no longer heard the music because Sgt. Santos was running up the front steps toward him, pointing in the direction that Davy had gone.

The Sergeant was huffing and puffing as he gave the chief bad news. "The Diogo girl has gotten into a car at the side entrance to the town hall on Ryder Street. I think Davy Souza is running after it toward the wharf." The police officer stopped to catch his breath.

James Crowley cursed. "Damn it." He looked in the direction that his sergeant pointed. He said, "Santos, get the patrol car. It's around back. Go after the car that Davy was chasing, the one the Diogo girl got into. I think they're heading for a boat. I'm going to get help from the Coast Guard." The chief stopped and turned around. "Keep the radio on in the car. Let me know if any boat leaves the dock. Use some kind of code. Say *the pigeons have left the coop*. Understand?" The chief was still hollering as he ran in the opposite direction. "Don't try to stop that boat by yourself. Be careful. These men are armed and dangerous."

Chief Crowley knew that the federal government had a sting operation in place. Their plan was to catch smugglers in the act. The police chief had been briefed about it a few days ago when Detective Shiff brought the FBI agent to his office. Government men were waiting for a boat to leave Provincetown Harbor heading for an offshore rendezvous. A Coast Guard Cutter was tied to Sklaroff's wharf, waiting to follow the vessel. Federal agents would handle the intercept.

They would confiscate the vessel and its cargo. Chief Crowley had no part in the operation.

Now a different intrigue was playing out, one that involved two innocent people. Crowley knew it would take him only a few minutes to get to the Coast Guard vessel. There wasn't a moment to loose. He headed west to the old pier that had suffered significant damage during the December gale. One of the buildings had been torn off its foundations by tremendous winds, but most of the pier was intact. The pilings, decking, and two other buildings remained standing. Four boats were tied to the end of the wharf, three fishing boats and one USCG Cutter, *Morrill*. The cutter had no particular markings, no nets hanging from the mast. It was polished, a new member to the fleet.

James Crowley stepped aboard this misplaced vessel. Uniformed men with guns holstered stood at attention on either side of the wheelhouse door. State Police Detective Charles Shiff and FBI Agent Joseph Amaral nodded when the policeman stepped over the threshold. Before the chief had a chance to speak the agent said, "I have men waiting below deck in the foc'sle. Has a boat left the wharf?" Chief Crowley was shaking his head, trying to catch his breath, adrenaline pumping throughout his body. The Federal Agent was unaware of Crowley's distress. He continued, "When that boat makes a move, we go." He was a just under six feet tall with a square chin and an intense look in his eyes as if he were on guard or stalking prey. He had been working steadily to make this night happen. For the past forty-eight hours he had been aboard the Coast Guard Cutter while waiting for word of the vessel's departure. The plan was to follow the vessel, keeping at a distance, to the rendezvoused site where Government agents were expecting a meeting with a freighter to take place. The coordinates would be radioed to the United States Navy. They were standing by, ready to move at a moment's notice. The US Navy would escort the foreign vessel to Boston. No one was absolutely sure what the cargo would be, but the FBI had word of guns, immigrants, and gold, perhaps all three.

"We want that boat to make its connection off shore. The Navy is waiting for my signal." The government agent was almost giddy with the thought of capturing spies and coins. "We are looking for a Dutch freighter, the mother ship. That is the prize."

Their plans did not include Mary Diogo or Davy Souza.

Chief Crowley held up his hands, palms out, to stop the federal agent. "You have to change your plans." He a took a deep breath, " Mary Diogo has been kidnapped. I believe she is aboard the boat that you are about to follow." He explained to the federal agent that the fisherman, Davy Souza, had gone running up the wharf after them and that his sergeant was also heading for the boat. "The car that took Mary Diogo is heading up Railroad Wharf. If what I'm thinking is correct, your smuggling operation and the man who killed Alonzo are one and the same. He is hoping to rid himself of any connections to Alonzo's murder — on their way out of the harbor." Chief Crowley looked around at the others. "He's got the Diogo girl. We have to stop that boat. Now." The others in the wheelhouse looked surprised and angry.

The sound of inspiration could be heard as Detective Shiff sucked in a deep breath. Then James Crowley's words exploded inside the small wheelhouse, "We can't wait. We have to go — now!"

"Damn it. Our nation's security is at risk. This is the entry point. This is our chance to catch them red handed." The men could hear the anger in Agent Amaral voice.

Crowley's voice boomed. "Mary Diogo's life is at stake." Chief Crowley leaned into the agents face. He was visibly shaken, "To hell with finding the rendezvous. We've got to stop that boat, if it isn't already too late."

At that moment the radio on the dashboard gave a squelch, crackling, interrupting the men, "This is Santos. The pigeons have flown." A pause and then, "Can you hear me? I repeat — the birds have left the coop."

The men in the wheelhouse looked at each other. "Damn," the word came from the Federal Agent's mouth like a rifle shot. "Yes, of course, of course. All right, Captain let go the lines. Take the boat out. Let's get after them." His voice was raspy, rough, and slightly hoarse like he'd smoked too many cigarettes or had been talking nonstop for days. He put his hat back on his head, pulled it down, and clenched his teeth. "Put the throttle down hard."

Chapter 21

When Davy Souza left the Town Hall the ballroom was filled with laughter and dancing, but he was filled with fear and dread. His stomach felt like it was in a vise. He couldn't stop to explain to Mr. Diogo who had approached him. Every second counted. He was hoping to catch up to Mary and stop her, but she had moved quickly from the auditorium. He ran after her, pushed open the side door, and burst into the cold night air. He was standing ten feet above street level watching Mary get into a black Packard car. A man in a topcoat and fedora hat was getting in behind her. He felt panic as he watched the car pulling away.

Davy didn't feel his feet hit the ground. He sprinted down the stairs, around the balustrade, and onto the path that led to the street. He kept running in the same direction the car was heading. When he reached the waterfront at the foot of Fishermen's Wharf he watched the black vehicle turn left and then right onto Railroad Wharf, a block away. During the past month the railroad tracks were being removed from this wharf. Piles of metal and debris slowed the car's progress as it made its way toward the end of the wharf. Davy needed to hurry.

Many wharfs ran parallel to each other, jutting into the harbor with a short distance of water between them. Davy ran straight ahead onto the wooden planks of Fishermen's Wharf. He could just make out the headlights of the car. It was the only vehicle moving. A half moon gave minimal light as Davy scanned his surroundings. Many boats dotted the horizon. A few skiffs lay turned over on the beach and a number of dories were tied to the wharf on trip-lines, a system of rope and pulley similar to the lines in back yards used to hang wet clothing.

The fisherman hurried over thick planks, worn and splintered from years of use, to the closest trip-line. A half-tide provided enough water so that the boat could be pulled close to the ladder. Luck was with him. The dory had oars. His hands shook as he untied the rope that held the dory to the dock. Leaving the line hanging on the ladder, he jumped into the dory. Saying a prayer, he began pulling on the oars with his powerful arms. His upper body muscles were straining beneath his Sunday suit.

Davy rowed with conviction and fervor, turning occasionally to keep the end of Railroad Wharf on the bow. He remembered the first time he rowed a dory when he was eight years old and how hard it had been. Now he was moving like the wind across the water. Wiping a bead of sweat from his upper lip, breathing out clouds of vapor, his heart was pounding in his chest. It felt as if he were eight years old again pulling the heavy skiff through the water for the first time, a test of endurance. Only now it was life or death.

He could hear the unusual sounds of music against the motionless night as the oars splashed into the water. His strokes eased as he drew nearer the main terminal. No trains, no cars, and no people could be seen on the wharf. On most nights the streets in town were deserted and quiet while the waterfront was alive with the coming and going of boats and the unloading of fish, but tonight everything had changed. The town was alive and the waterfront unusually quiet. The night air was frigid and still.

In the distance Davy could see an eerie sea smoke, a low-lying fog that forms when sea temperatures are considerably higher than the cold air flowing over it. Listening for sounds where none should be, the fisherman heard the muffled throaty cough of a Detroit diesel engine coming to life at the end of the wharf. He hurried, rowing toward the familiar sound. His heart beat faster as he rowed. If the dory bumped against the vessel it could alert the crew, so when he reached the boat he kept it at arms length while he looked around. The car that had taken Mary was parked on the dock next to the boat. There was no driver and its engine was turned off. He knew with certainty that this vessel was not a Provincetown dragger. It was rigged to go fishing with nets hanging from the mast and gear lying on the stern deck, but everything looked new, unused and a bit staged. He heard the sound of an engine and then muffled voices that came from the wheelhouse. He couldn't make out the words, but the tone was unmistakable, commanding, rushed and loud.

Davy didn't have a plan. He stepped onto the dory's seat and then placed his foot into the ship's scupper, pushing the small boat away from the side of the trawler, letting it drift with the tide. With a heave up, he jumped over the rail landing with a soft thud. Nothing stirred. This boat had a Western rig. The placement of the wheelhouse was forward, above where he thought the foc'sle would be. He headed for a small door under the wheelhouse, hoping it would lead him below deck, and to his childhood friend. Was he in time? Would Mary be there? Was she hurt? These

217

thoughts ran through his mind as he turned the cold metal handle of the doorway. Then suddenly something hard struck the back of his head. He fell, stunned, unconscious before he hit the deck.

There was a pounding behind his eyes when he opened them. His arms were tied behind his back and he was lying on his side in a moving boat. He rolled over. Mary lay next to him. He could feel the terror rising in his throat when he saw that her mouth had been gagged. His heart went cold. He looked into her wide eyes and immediately began to move to her, wriggling like a snake. He whispered, "Come close, I'll pull the gag from your mouth with my teeth." They wiggled around until his mouth was close enough to pull the handkerchief out. "Mary, are you all right?"

"Thank God you're alive," she said as she gasped for air.

"We've got to get out of here," Davy whispered. He tried pulling unsuccessfully at the rope that bound his wrists. "Can you turn around? Move your body. Put your back toward me. I'll try to get you untied." They began to roll, twist and move around the cabin floor while the boat swayed slowly, side to side, heading away from land to open water. "If I can untie you we have a good chance." Whether or not it was true didn't matter, he gave her hope.

She was wiggling, inching forward. "Davy, why are they doing this? What's this all about? What do they want?" Her voice was just this side of hysterical, high pitched, almost shrill.

"Shh, quiet, Mary. We don't want them to hear us," he whispered. "With the engine running I don't think they can. We seem to be in the foc'sle, in front of the engine room. The wheelhouse is above us."

Mary paused, hiccupped, stifling her words so that she sounded as if she were choking. She whispered, "I was told by my friend Susan that my aunt and uncle from Boston were here to surprise my parents." She stopped and muffled a sob. "She said that Aunt Ellen and Uncle Randy were waiting in a car for me."

"Never mind that now, Mary, how long have I been out?" Davy was trying to loosen the rope holding Mary's arms behind her back. "How long has the boat been underway?" He tried to be gentle but the worry in his voice was unmistakable. As they talked he felt the knot loosen.

"Not long." Her voice cracked. He felt her tears against his neck when she turned her head to get closer. "I've lost track of time but I think we've been underway for only a few minutes." Her words were barely audible. The cabin was dark. Portholes threw a silver light into the room, revealing only shadows as they felt their way around each other.

"Hold still. I'm getting the knot undone. The stupid guy used a half-hitch." His fingers were strong from working with twine and fish net all his life. "I'm not sure what this is all about, but I have a feeling it has something to do with Alonzo. Have they asked you anything?" The two strained, back to back, looking for answers while struggling to free themselves.

"No. No one has spoken to me. Davy, I'm so frightened. They put something over my face. I woke up as they carried me aboard. They have guns. I saw one in a holster under the man's arm." She began to cry.

Davy said, "Hush Mary, You're loose." The couple turned to face each other. He continued, "We must be getting close to Long Point. It's the closest we'll get to land. The water is shallow near the tip of the point. Quick, untie me."

As Mary worked to free his hands, he continued to reassure her. "If I can get to the wheelhouse, maybe I can put the boat up on the bar." They were rubbing their wrists, looking at each other, their faces just inches apart. "Do you remember how many were on board? Did you see who brought you here?" Davy wanted to know what they were up against even if he didn't have a plan.

"I should never have left the town hall." She took a deep breath, "Oh I don't know what I was thinking. I was stupid."

Davy put his arm around her. "Sh-sh, you're not stupid. Please, tell me what you remember. How many men?"

She whispered, "I saw one man in the wheelhouse and the one that was carrying me, but there may be another, I'm not sure."

Her pupils expanded to dark round orbs. She had no doubt that they were about to die. "They tied my hands, stuffed a rag in my mouth, and put me in here."

He pulled her closer then up onto her feet. "Come on, we've got to find a way out." Metallic light from the moon-glow fluttered across the room outlining bunks in the forepeak, a table, and a short ladder that led to a closed door in the ceiling. "Those steps lead to the wheelhouse," he whispered. "They'll be in there. We can't go that way, not much chance of surprising them." Davy looked around. "There's a small hatchway toward the engine room. I think it will take me out onto the stern of the boat. The engine noise will cover any sounds that I make. You wait here." He knew he would have to make his way to the wheelhouse from outside, across an open deck. Whatever it took, whatever the cost, it was their only chance.

Mary interrupted his thoughts. "No way," she hissed. "You are not leaving me here. I'm going with you. I'll be right behind you." He didn't try to dissuade her. The note of determination in her voice kept him silent. He was thinking of the layout of the boat as Mary put her hand on his back and held onto his coattail. She followed him to a small door that led to the engine room. Davy stopped and Mary bumped against him. "Step over the sill," he mouthed and pointed down. His head was pounding from the blow he'd taken. Bending, they stepped into a passageway where a single light bulb illuminated a Detroit diesel engine. No other sound could be heard above the rumbling. He took her hand and placed it on a pipe handrail. She grabbed the pipe with her right hand and clutched the back of his clothing with the left, afraid to let go of either. He put his index finger to his lips, a signal without need of explanation. A small room containing the engineer's quarters came next. Davy knew they would have to cross it to get to the steps that led to the stern deck. He opened the hatchway door slowly. One light bulb hung from the center of the room. It contained a bunk with a folded wool blanket and nothing else.

On the opposite side of the empty compartment three steps led to a wooden door. Half expecting someone to be waiting, standing outside, he turned the handle with trepidation. Adrenaline was now pumping through his veins, his anger building. He took a deep breath and felt Mary's hand clutching his jacket behind him. He heard a sigh of relief, realizing it came from him when he opened the door. No one was there. He could see the Provincetown skyline, stars, and the dunes above the cove. They were still inside the harbor and closing on Long Point. That was a good thing. It meant they hadn't reached the end of land yet. They would pass the tip of the point soon. They had to hurry.

He led Mary behind a stack of wooden boxes next to the doghouse that they had just come out of. Davy peered around the boxes, looking across the boat. On the wall near the stairs leading to the wheelhouse he saw an ax. He felt a glimmer of hope. With a bit of luck, he'd surprise the men at the wheel, gain control of the helm, and head the boat for the wharf or onto the sandbar. They crouched behind the boxes while Davy contemplated his next move.

Twelve-feet away, across an open deck, stairs on both the port and starboard led to the wheelhouse. He could see a red light glowing on the inside where two men in silhouette were standing stiffly, swaying, appearing like cutout characters from a cartoon. If there was a third man, he was nowhere to be seen. Davy planned to grab the ax as he moved to the starboard stairway that would take him into the wheelhouse. Surprise was on his side.

"Mary, stay here, no questions. And no, you are not coming with me. I have to work fast if I'm going to stop this boat. Watch for my signal when I get control." Davy spoke in a calm voice. "If something goes wrong I want you to head up the stairs on the port side. There is a ladder that will take you to the roof and the life raft." He gave her his pocketknife. "It may be your only escape." She nodded her understanding. A look passed between them. "Use the raft if you have too, you know what I mean." He looked into her eyes. "If I don't get back to you." There was more to be said, but they had run out of time. "Mary," he said, but he didn't finish the sentence. Instead he kissed her lightly on the mouth and ran across the open deck to where the ax was fixed to the wall.

Davy grew up in Provincetown sprinting down beaches, through alleyways, and across town streets. He was fast. He had been on the school track team. But this time he was not quick enough. A shot rang out, loud and sharp. Mary flinched, jumping at the sound. The flash against the darkness illuminated the figure of a man with a gun in his hand. And then she saw Davy fall. She wanted to run to him, but was paralyzed. She couldn't catch up to the scene before her. It was happening as if in a dream. It couldn't be real. Mary watched the two men in the wheelhouse turn around at the sound of the gun's detonation. From the opposite side of the vessel a third man stepped out from the shadows, holding the railing of the metal stairway on the port side that led to the deck. He was heading toward Davy.

There are times in one's life that actions take on another dimension, as if you have no control over them. You are propelled by a source greater than yourself. Her friend had risked his life to come after her and he was now lying on the deck. His body was moving, synchronized with the rolling of the boat, as if he were a log or dead seal. The man with the gun, wearing a fedora hat pulled down to his eyebrows, moved toward Davy. He was swaying in an odd way, stumbling sideways, trying to stand straight while pocketing the gun. The man's movements were spastic like a drunken sailor, unable to coordinate his feet with the swaying boat. There was no doubt about his intentions for the fallen man. The railing was only a few steps away. He bent over the unconscious fisherman. He was going to throw Davy into the water.

The impulse to move had nothing to do with rational thought. Mary's hand fell on a gaff, a short handled oak club with a large hook in the end. She took it from its place, holding it above her head, and ran at the killer as he was lifting Davy. She hit him across his back with all the force she could muster. The blow didn't kill him, but it caught him off guard. He dropped Davy and stumbled, lurching in disharmony against the boat's rolling motion. His body hit the rail. At the same time, as if lightening had struck, spotlights came on, and everyone beheld a scene that would later be described as unbelievable.

Time moved in slow motion. It was as if they were watching a Humphrey Bogart movie, unreal, and yet happening before their eyes. It was a scene not likely to be forgotten. Mary was still gripping the club in both hands above her head, as if unable to let go. She was screaming as the man in the long coat, arms flailing, hit the gunwale at hip level just as the boat rolled into a swell. He fell into the dark water, disappearing from view.

The U. S. Coast Guard had arrived. Crewmen on the rescue boat ran to the railing. Mary dropped the gaff and went to Davy who lay unconscious on the deck. He was moving from side to side with the motion of the boat. From somewhere above her head, a commanding voice using a megaphone said, "This is the United States Coast Guard. Prepare to be boarded." A machine gun was fired into the night sky.

Mary was on her knees, pulling Davy's body to her, bringing his shoulders onto her lap, cradling him. "Davy, Davy, Davy," she cried. Her words were swallowed by the sound of the water, engines, and men hollering. Her cry was absorbed into the night sky as she held the fisherman.

For a second time the words echoed, loud, calm, and ordered. "Captain, this is an order by the United States Coast Guard. Take your vessel out of gear. I repeat, this is the United States Coast Guard, prepare to be boarded." The Coast Guard vessel was alongside in seconds. Two guardsmen tied ropes to the cleats as others stood at the rail with guns drawn. The two men in the seized boat's wheelhouse stepped out with their hands stretched high above their heads. Coast

Guardsmen pointed their guns at the men as they made their way down the steps and onto the deck.

Mary began screaming when she saw blood coming from Davy. All eyes turned to her as she pleaded, "Help him, please. Help him." Her small body was vibrating like the wings of a hummingbird when a blanket was placed around her shoulders. She was lifted to her feet, away from her friend as others took control. Mary looked up into the face of James Crowley as he put his arm around her shoulder. His voice was calm, choked with emotion as he spoke, "It's over Mary. You're safe now." The daughter of his best friend put her head on his chest and cried.

Davy was wrapped in a wool blanket, lifted onto a stretcher, and transported across the railings to the Coast Guard Cutter. He was whisked away before Mary had time to say goodbye. Mary, Chief Crowley, Detective Shiff and Agent Amaral watched from the deck of the confiscated fishing trawler as the coast guard vessel headed, full throttle, toward town.

There was a scramble to retrieve the man who had fallen overboard. Life rings were tossed, searchlights scanned across the water, and a boathook was used to pick up a hat that floated behind the boat. There was no sign of the man. It is believed that he was sucked down, into the propeller when he entered the water.

Chapter 22

The ride back to Railroad Wharf in the captured trawler was slow and steady. An officer took Mary to the galley area where she and Davy had been held prisoner. She shivered and pulled the blanket tighter when she saw the ropes that had tied their hands. She had wanted to stay with Davy, but was not given a choice. Chief Crowley told her to go below until they were back at the wharf. Shock was beginning to hit her as she sat at the small table, thought about what had happened, and cried. She had killed a man.

Meanwhile on deck, the prisoners were handcuffed and sat on overturned fish boxes in the stern. Coast Guard crewmen watched over them with guns at the ready. Neither man had said a word.

In the wheelhouse James Crowley, Charles Shiff, and Joseph Amaral crowded next to the uniformed officer as he steered the boat back to Provincetown. A dim red light glowed in the compass, reflecting on their serious faces as they recounted the night's events. Treason was mentioned, as well as illegal aliens, spies, and gold.

Agent Amaral was the first to speak. "I'm hoping our Navy will find the freighter that these fellows were on their way to meet." He sighed and then told them how their plan had developed. "Our Washington office was notified in December when two men were picked up during a protest in New York City. They were found with forged documents." There had been numerous strikes around the country. In Boston and New York marches were organized, gathering people together to protest the long hours, poor wages, and unsafe working conditions. "At one particular event dock workers began pushing, shoving, and getting the mob worked up."

The federal agent held himself erect, shoulders square, chin jutting out, giving the impression that he was secure in both his knowledge and leadership. He continued speaking, "The police were called to disperse the crowd. They did what was necessary and used what was needed, Billy clubs and horses. You know how it is. There were injuries. People were taken off in ambulances and paddy-wagons." The agent waited for questions that didn't come. Amaral looked through the wheelhouse windows and continued his story. "For the bureau this was just another protest against labor, management and banks," said the FBI agent. "There is plenty of socialist rhetoric out there: replace freedom with a government system of control. Fascists and radicals, if you ask me." The agent hesitated, as if deciding how much to tell. "But then, a New York City police officer picked up two men during the protest. There was something funny about the passport photos. Closer inspection revealed forgeries, good ones, and we got a call."

Everyone waited. The boat rolled with an easy sway. The men listened to the hum of the engines and watched the lights from town grow larger. Amaral went on, "Immigrants are always welcome in America. You men know that. But we don't need people causing protests, riots, and stopping production." His loyalty was unquestionable. "And we sure don't need subversives who are hell-bent on mayhem and destruction. A bomb planted in New York not long ago killed two innocent women. We're pretty sure Bolsheviks were responsible."

Amaral's voice was husky like he'd been talking for days without stopping. "I know you'll keep what I'm telling you under your hats." He touched the brim of his and then said, "Our agency was given information by these same two men in exchange for leniency. They told us about immigrants and gold coming into the country from Germany, onboard a merchant ship from Copenhagen." He let this sink in. "I came to Boston to meet Detective Shiff when I learned that Shiff was looking for information about a ship from Copenhagen that stopped in Provincetown in late October. I called Detective Shiff and he told me about the murder of Alonzo and the gold coin that the immigrant gave to his girlfriend. For the past few weeks our team has been searching for the smugglers.

Their trail lead us to Provincetown." He smiled. Chief Crowley thought he looked like the Cheshire cat in *Alice's Adventures in Wonderland*.

The FBI agent spoke again, this time about certain people, boats and trucks moving in and out of Provincetown. "At first our agency didn't see the death of Alonzo as part of our bigger picture. We assumed a jealous boyfriend, or husband murdered him. When the fish buyer was murdered we began to suspect that there was a connection to the smuggling operation." The men in the wheelhouse listened to the federal agent explain more. "At one point we thought that the fish buyer might be the person transporting the illegal goods, but that turns out not be true. The man responsible for trucking the immigrants around the country was Carlos Suvera. He needed to get rid of Alonzo because Alonzo knew about the ship that was bringing in the illegal contraband. We learned that Suvera was the connection to the offshore operation and that's what we've been after." The agent looked at Chief Crowley and said, "It turns out that your murderer and my smuggler were one and the same."

The FBI agent continued, "Our priority was not a local murder, but the welfare of our country." The agent took off his hat and ran his hand through his hair, "I'm hoping our plans will still work. Our Navy is searching for the freighter. If we find it, we'll escort it to Boston Harbor and go through it with a fine toothed comb."

The gold coins were on everyone's mind. The agent didn't disappoint, "Our thinking is that Carlos knew about the two stolen coins. They were a link to him. He wanted them. He wasn't going to leave them behind. And maybe there are more, we don't know yet." The agent was on a roll and had everyone's attention. "As far as Mary Diogo was concerned, well, she was a loose end who might know too much about Carlos and his business. Alonzo may have told her things and Suvera wasn't going to take any chances." The federal agent surprised everyone when he said, "Well gentlemen, I'd like to thank for your help."

The federal agent appeared proud when he said, "We've been keeping the German National Socialist Workers Union under surveillance. These people preach a totalitarian form of government where one state, or one party or one man, namely Hitler has total control, omnipotent, with absolute power." He finished with, "We can't be too careful when it comes to our freedom."

The federal agent did not repeat the rumors he had heard circulating around Washington. It was said that some people believed Germany had plans to infiltrate the United States of America. There was talk of refugees and gold coming into the country in order to begin building the Third Reich here in the states.

Amaral thought about what it would mean if a steady stream of smuggled men and women with orders from Hitler were to infiltrate our shores. He had heard that the man, Hitler, was quite mad. If the dictator was sending people to American to disrupt our way of life, usurp freedom by bringing unrest, or worse, terrorists and killers into America, well then Agent Amaral would do everything in his power to stop it.

Chief Crowley interrupted the federal agent's thoughts. "That reminds me of a something I read recently by Sir J. E. Dalberg," Chief Crowley said, *"Power tends to corrupt and absolute power corrupts absolutely."* The Provincetown policeman liked adding his two cents to the conversation. The others nodded in agreement.

It took half an hour for the boat to reach Railroad Wharf. Mary, shaken and exhausted was delivered to her parents who had waited with Officer Santos in the patrol car on the wharf. He drove them home after an emotional reunion. The three law-enforcement officials went directly to Chief Crowley's office. The prisoners were held by the Coast Guard aboard the cutter to be transported to Boston in the morning. The Fishermen's Ball was over, leaving the cold snowy streets deserted as the clock in the town hall tower struck two. The men descended into the basement office. The Boston detective suggested a debriefing to wrap things up. They were showing signs of fatigue, but coffee and adrenaline kept them going.

Chief Crowley turned to face the other two as he sat behind his desk. "I won't be charging Mary of course. She couldn't have known the man would be pitched into the sea, and she was defending herself. As far as I'm concerned she should be getting a medal."

Detective Shiff replied, "She's lucky to be alive." He changed the subject and asked, "Can I use your phone for a quick call?" Crowley nodded. Shiff picked up the telephone and gave the operator a number. He mumbled a few words, listened briefly and then hung up. "I've got some good news for you chief." He was a man of few words, but when he did speak it came out rapidly as if he needed to get everything summed up and over with as quickly as possible so he could move on. "My men searched Carlos Suvera's truck and rooms after he left for the dance this evening. Suvera took his touring car, the Packard, and left his trucks on the street near his rooming house. That phone call I just made informed me that a knife was found under the driver's seat wrapped in a hand towel. It has blood on it."

The Boston Detective looked at Crowley, smiled, and continued, "The knife has gone to the medical examiner. I have a feeling it will match the wounds on both your victims. I'll know more in a couple of days, but I was told that it looks to be the right size and

shape. You have your killer, even if he is a dead one."
The Boston detective pulled three cigars out of his coat
pocket. "Not very smart of him to keep it." He shook
his head. "Just shows how cocky he was." He offered
the other men a cigar.

The federal agent interrupted, "I'll call Washington
and let them know what we've been up to tonight. All
ships in the vicinity of Boston will be scrutinized over
the next few days. And I think we'll get all kinds of
useful information from the captain and crewmen
from the trawler." He lit a match and puffed on the
Cuban cigar. "Looks like we've had ourselves quite an
evening." He laughed along with Detective Shiff and
Chief Crowley.

"It seems we missed the big dance," Chief Crowley
tugged at his mustache. "I hope we'll be around to
enjoy the next one. That's if Hitler doesn't get his way
and move into Washington." Everyone laughed. They
couldn't foresee the United States being drawn into a
war on the other side of the Atlantic, much less the
man actually having influence within our borders.
Everyone was underestimating the avarice, hatred, and
power behind the dictator.

The three men were not yet ready to leave the small
warm office. A pot of coffee was produced, cups passed
around, and the talk became sporadic. As he puffed on
the Havana, Chief Crowley wondered if the cigar had
come from Carlos's supply. He saw it as ironic,

enjoying a cigar brought to town by a now dead murderer. His thoughts returned to the talk of war in Europe. "Roosevelt has said that our government has a policy of no interference. I used to think that we'd be better off not interfering, give Germany what they want and keep the peace. But now I'm not so sure." No one in the room knew that Hitler's Army would grow, march across Europe, and decimate whole populations of people. What they did know was that they had kept their world safe, at least for the time being.

A wave of sedition had passed through America's cities. Rebellion added fuel to the flames of unrest that was spreading like a wild fire in scorching summer, but at the same time it was bringing out facts about working conditions and poverty within our country. The attention of the public was on the workers of America, not on war in Europe or Asia. While the country wrestled within itself the inner structure our government debated the world as a whole, and waited, hoping to see peace restored both within and outside the United States. No one wanted war.

The three men in the basement office had been given a glimpse into the difficulties and realities of keeping the peace in our country. Their experience tonight had opened their eyes to the potential danger of infiltration by sea.

Agent Amaral said, "I've been thinking about what would happen if money sent by Hitler was given to a group of hand picked, English speaking German citizens along with plans to move into cities around the country, assimilate, take on positions of power, run the banks, run for political offices, and wait for orders. It gives me the willies." He puffed on the cigar.

The three men sat in silence, alone with their own thoughts. The murder of Alonzo was not part of a love triangle, as Chief Crowley had believed. The chief admitted to himself that he was wrong, but he would not admit it to anyone else, not to the FBI, the State Police, or to his friend Manny, and certainly not to Davy Souza. Common sense and police procedure had pointed him toward Davy. While the Provincetown police chief had kept an eye on Davy, Davy was following Mary like a guard dog. While the town was planning a fishermen's ball, the FBI was getting closer to men who were traitors to our country. Chief Crowley now felt he could rely on these two men should he ever again need their help. And he hoped he never would.

Agent Amaral interrupted the police chief thoughts, "The security of the United States takes precedence over everything else," Agent Amaral said. The man blew out a veil of smoke. "Provincetown held the key all along." No one expected that the Diogo girl would be targeted and they didn't count on Davy Souza at all. Everyone on the government team was taken by surprise. It had been a close call.

"I think I'll call the hospital about Davy Souza." The men all stood up, replacing their topcoats. They shook hands before leaving. Dawn was breaking when they left the basement office, stepping into a new day.

Two weeks later Detective Shiff showed up at the Provincetown Police Station with information for Crowley. "I thought you'd be happy to hear that the medical examiner has confirmed that the weapon found in the truck belonging to Carlos Suvera was definitely your murder weapon."

There was a moment of silence, then a sigh of relief. James sat back in his chair. The February weather was frigid. The office was hot. The only call the police had had in the past week was from Mrs. Reis who said the crows were outside her chicken coop making a racket and she wanted a policeman to come to her house and get rid of the birds. She said she needed protection for her six chickens. James was glad that the town was quiet.

Crowley tried to keep his thoughts about Mary, Alonzo, and Davy to a minimum, but when Detective Shiff was seated in his office he said, "When I questioned Mary the first time about Alonzo, I was sure that she didn't know more than she had told me. She gave me details regarding Alonzo's life and I felt she didn't know anything else." He shook his head, looked across the desk at the Boston detective, and said, "Mary was a very lucky loose end." She hadn't told him everything, the sin of omission, leaving out important details. "Mary knew the name of the ship, where it was from and what it was carrying. If she had been honest with us from the beginning she wouldn't have seen Davy Souza shot while saving her life," Crowley said. She had come very close to losing everything and they both knew it. Chief Crowley continued, "My interrogation techniques have been sharpened by what transpired here." The chief smiled. "I also think you should have told me sooner what you were up to and who you suspected. We might have saved ourselves a boat trip, and I could have danced at the Fishermen's Ball."

The Boston detective's head bobbed in the affirmative and chuckled. "Well I guess we've both learned a few things. I wanted you to know that the feds have put together a nasty picture of Carlos Suvera." Detective Shiff said. "He was wanted in New York City in connection with another murder. There is an ongoing investigation into the death of a man thrown out of a window from five stories up. The feds think he was a cold blooded assassin."

The Boston detective continued, "I was told by Agent Amaral that the whiskey salesman was paid to ingratiate himself into your community, learn what he could about Alonzo and find the stolen Prussian coins. They had to eliminate any connection to the Dutch freighter. Then Carlos Suvera learned that Jimmy-the-fish-buyer exchanged money for the gold coin. He was another potential threat." The chief nodded, said nothing. "Carlos discovered that Alonzo was staying onboard the fishing boat *Annabella R.* instead of returning to his room on Bradford Street. He slipped onto the boat, killed Alonzo, and dumped the body over the side." Detective Shiff added, "After he took care of Alonzo, he went after the coins."

The Boston detective told Chief Crowley the details of Alonzo's death. Statements had been taken from the men who worked for Carlos. The captain of the confiscated boat told the police he just ran the boat and didn't have anything to do with murder. He told the Boston detective that Carlos laughed when he killed Alonzo because he thought the fisherman was praying to the Holy Virgin. Before he died, Alonzo called out the name, "Mary." Chief Crowley decided he would not share that information with anyone.

Chief Crowley stood, "I need a breath of fresh air. Come on I'll buy you lunch over at the Mayflower Cafe." He told the desk Sargent that he and Detective Shiff were going out for lunch.

After the meal the two officers went their separate ways. Shiff headed back to Boston and Chief Crowley inhaled the salt air as he walked Commercial Street. The police chief thought about Alonzo being dragged from his bunk in the middle of the night with a knife at his throat, without his boots or coat. He was most likely searched and questioned. He must have told Carlos that he had traded the coins to the old man, a fish buyer named Jimmy. When Carlos found only one coin he began thinking about Alonzo's girlfriend and the family that had rescued him.

Carlos Suvera was wrong about a lot of things. He was wrong about the strength and direction of the tides, assuming the body would be taken out to sea, around the tip of the point to deeper water, never to be seen again. He was wrong about the people in Provincetown, that good guys were willing to go to their deaths to defend what is right. And he was wrong about the lengths a man will go to protect the woman he loves.

Chief Crowley thought it was ironic that he had never met Alonzo and yet he felt he knew him. A wave of pity swept over him for the dead man, like the tide rushing for the beach. He was certain that Alonzo could have found a place among the town's independent fishermen, if he hadn't become involved with the wrong people, on the wrong ship, going in the wrong direction.

Chapter 23

The soft zephyrs of spring had replaced winter gales. Sea gulls drifted on air currents outside the Diogo family's kitchen window on a bright morning in May. Around the table sat Manny, Eleanor, Mary, and Chief Crowley. The chief had made it a point to stop in for a cup of coffee whenever he could, to say hello and keep up with the family news. Manny Diogo was now buying coffee beans and grinding them in the evening to sell to the fishermen at a nice profit. Crowley sipped the rich brew and smiled, he'd never tasted better. He had come to their home today because he had something important to give to Mary. Chief Crowley put his hand inside his jacket pocket and took out a small box. "Mary, I believe this belongs to you," he said.

Mary took the box and lifted the lid. All eyes fell on the shinning gold coin. No one spoke as the teakettle began to hiss with steam. Waves breaking against the shore could be heard, and then a knock at the kitchen door caused everyone to look away from the coin. In walked Davy Souza. Eleanor jumped up. "Sit here, Davy. You're looking very healthy this morning." She pulled a chair out for him.

Chief Crowley stood and shook hands with the young fisherman, "Glad to see you, Davy. You look fit."

Davy greeted the chief, "Total recovery, so they tell me." He then asked the policeman about the freighter that was supposed to be involved in smuggling. "Have they found it?"

"Yes, and I've learned that it was a Dutch freighter, the *Zuiderdijk*. It was escorted to Boston the day after our raid on the trawler. The ship has been impounded by the Coast Guard." Everyone was quiet. Crowley continued, "Three men and a woman were arrested, but no gold coins were found. I was told that the first mate laughed out loud when asked about a shipment of gold coins. He told the FBI agents that he and the captain threw the treasure overboard when they saw the lights from the Navy ship."

Everyone around the kitchen table thought about treasure and what it could mean. "The arresting federal officers figured that they either had the wrong boat or that no such gold existed." Crowley shrugged his shoulders and added, "Who knows?"

"A cargo of Jamaican rum and boxes with cans of sardines heading for Boston's legal seafood market were found in the vessel's cargo hold." Chief Crowley looked at Davy. "Turns out that the three men and one woman were German Jews fleeing the tyranny sweeping across their country. They had paid the captain to

243

bring them to America. We'll let the federal government sort that out. The crewmen onboard the vessel had passports from France, all appeared legal.

Chief Crowley was glad to be the bearer of good news. He smiled and added, "I'm sure all their names will be added to the list that the feds keep on file somewhere in government offices. I don't think anyone knows how this will affect us in the long run." No questions were asked, but everyone nodded. Chief Crowley looked at Davy and added, "I think Carlos was planning that the deaths of Alonzo and Jimmy would be blamed on you. It seemed reasonable at the time. No offence, Davy."

"None taken," the fishermen said. His eyes flashed as he smiled, giving the police chief a fleeting glance into the man Davy had become.

The police chief continued, "Carlos was afraid that Mary might reveal a name that could unravel his plans. Any connection to him and the smuggling operation had to be severed. He was involved in more than murder." James Crowley looked around the small room. His eyes fell on his friend Manny. "Carlos wasn't about to take any chances, it was supposed to be an easy job for him." He was silent for a heartbeat then added, "If Davy hadn't seen Mary leave the dance or if the feds hadn't been watching for smugglers, God knows what could have happened."

An image of her bound and gagged and dumped in the cold Atlantic, disappearing on the way out to sea, a loose end, came to Crowley's mind. There was a pause in the conversation. It was time to give thanks while the world ordered itself.

Eleanor lifted everyone's thoughts and spirits when she said, "It was the coin that turned the tide, but it was love that saved our Mary." Davy blushed and looked at the table. Mary looked at her mother, but no one spoke. They could hear the surf outside the open window.

Davy Souza looked at his friends and smiled. A flash of regret registered in his eyes as he looked at the coin in the box on the table. He hesitantly said, "I came by today to let you know that I've signed up with Uncle Sam, joined the Navy. I'll be leaving in a few weeks for basic training." The family burst into exclamations, gathering around him, patting him on the back, and congratulating him.

Mary's bottom lip quivered. She took a deep breath, but did not shed a tear. She had known what he was going to tell her parents. A richer, deeper feeling of trust and friendship had developed between them. They would get a chance to say goodbye when she and Davy were alone.

Manny shook the fisherman's hand and said, "Good luck son." Each person in Eleanor's kitchen that morning was wondering about the future. Destiny was waiting.

Davy stood up and walked toward the door. He looked at Mary. She took a sweater from the coat rack and followed him out. Her parents did not ask where she was going.

Chief Crowley said goodbye to his friends and left by the door leading to the shop. A sense of satisfaction caused him to stop in the hallway and look back over his shoulder. Eleanor and Manny were standing close, arms around each other, looking out the kitchen window. The bell jingled when Crowley closed the door of the ship chandlery. He was smiling as he crossed Commercial Street and headed for his basement office.

96976673R00152

Made in the USA
Columbia, SC
06 June 2018